FLIGHT OF THE DRAGON

A DRAGON RIDERS OF ELANTIA NOVEL

JESSICA DRAKE

If you want to be notified when Jessica's next novel is released and get access to exclusive contests, giveaways, and freebies, sign up for her mailing list here. Your email address will never be shared and you can unsubscribe at any time.

❀ Created with Vellum

1

"This is ridiculous, Zara."

I winced as Lessie shot me a baleful glare from the floor. She was curled up on top of a pile of hay—a makeshift bed in a makeshift stable that had been converted from a saloon, the door torn out so she could fit through. It had only been a day since we'd left Zuar City, but the room had already taken on the same musty scent of the stables back home. Which in itself wouldn't be so bad if Lessie wasn't forced to stay indoors round the clock.

"I'm sorry," I said, sitting down next to her in the hay. I ran my hand over the iridescent scales on the side of her neck, gleaming like sapphires in the lamplight. "I wish I could take you above, Lessie, I really do. But we can't chance someone spotting you on deck."

"I am a dragon," Lessie huffed. "It is not in my nature to cower inside the belly of a ship. And it is certainly beneath my dignity to be flying inside a ship when I could be flying outside."

I smiled, scratching behind the crown of spikes protruding from her head. *"I know."* She tried to resist my touch, holding fiercely onto the grumpy attitude that had been brewing inside her these past twenty-four hours. *"But it won't be like this forever. Tavarian says we're landing in a couple of hours."*

"Are we?" A kernel of excitement bloomed in Lessie's heart, echoing my own. She craned her neck to look through the port-hole—her only view of the outside world. But her mood immediately soured when the only thing she saw was a world of fog. *"Hmph,"* she said, laying her head back down in the hay. *"Wake me when we arrive."*

I snorted, a smile twitching at my lips. Lessie had the soul of a grumpy old man and the heart of a toddler, highly intelligent and capricious all at once. Sometimes she was wise beyond her years, other times petulant and even bossy. The combination would have driven me crazy in a human, but as a dragon, she was utterly endearing.

I wonder if that's because of the dragon rider bond, I thought as I left Lessie's room and headed for the saloon. Would I feel the same way about Kadryn or Ykos if I had to spend a week with one of them instead, and they could communicate with me?

The thought of Jallis's and Rhia's dragons gave me a pang of homesickness. I'd only known them for a few months, but already I felt as if they were part of my little family. The thought of being holed up at some secret estate with only Tavarian for human company was a bit depressing, even though he was fasci-nating in his own right. I'd been told I could write to them, but that wasn't the same as actually curling up on one of the common room couches, talking about our lessons and pondering our dreams and futures.

Speaking of Tavarian... I entered the saloon to find him sitting at one of the tables. He had a cup of tea in one hand and a thick leather tome in the other, with several more stacked on the table in front of him. *History texts,* I thought as I tilted my head to study one of the titles.

"Ah. Miss Kenrook." Tavarian shut the book and gestured at the chair across from him. "Sit."

I did, leaning back in the chair and crossing my legs at the ankles. "Are you finally going to tell me where we are going?" I was pretty good at navigation, but we were flying high through thick clouds, and I'd barely managed to get a glimpse of the ground.

Tavarian raised his eyebrows. "You already know we're going to one of my estates," he said. "What more do you need to know?"

I rolled my eyes. "Maybe I don't *need* to know, but it would be nice to have some details. Are we going to another floating island? Some kind of bunker? Will there be an opportunity for me to do any treasure hunting?"

Tavarian's silver eyes flashed. "This is not a vacation or an expedition, Miss Kenrook," he said. "I am taking you into hiding from this unfortunate character you have chosen to ally yourself with so you and Lessie can continue to train in relative safety. As I am devoting myself to training you full time, you should be able to finish much faster than the average academy student."

My heart leaped despite the clear rebuke in his words. "Really?" I asked, unable to keep the eagerness out of my voice. "How much faster?"

"We may be able to cut it down to a year." Tavarian gave me a small smile, pleased at the change in my tone. "Once you're finished, you'll be able to start your military service."

Those last two words deflated my optimism faster than a spear thrown into a hot air balloon. "About that," I said carefully, preparing myself for a fight. "Is there any way to get out of it?"

"Out of what?"

"My military service."

Tavarian was silent for a moment. "Why?"

I took a deep breath. "Because I don't believe in fighting wars that I don't support," I said in a rush. "From everything I've studied, Elantia has spent the last thousand years throwing its weight around and bullying our surrounding neighbors into submission instead of working to establish real alliances. Nationalism is all good, but this idea that we're superior to everyone else just because we have dragons is asking for trouble. I don't want to risk my life or Lessie's just because my government can't pull its head out of its ass long enough to realize that it might not be the biggest power in the region anymore."

I expected Tavarian to scold or berate me, to be angry or disgusted at my lack of patriotism. But to my surprise, he sighed and set down his cup of tea.

"You are right," he said, and I nearly toppled out of my chair.

"Elantia has not been particularly kind to its neighbors since the Dragon War. Lord Lyton and I have been attempting to repair relations and establish trade again, and while we have had some success, several countries would still love nothing more than to crush us. I do not personally support the use of dragons in combat, not when we could invest our resources into upgrading our warfare technology, but tradition will not be denied. Thankfully, it has been a good while since Elantia has made war on another country, and we have no plans to do so in the near future. My hope is that Lyton's and my efforts will continue to improve relations, and that you and Lessie will come out of your ten years of service relatively unscathed."

"I...what?" I gaped at him. "You mean I don't have to be stuck in the military for the rest of my life?"

"Of course not." Tavarian didn't smile, but there was a distinct twinkle of amusement in his eyes. "How do you think we dragon riders managed to get so wealthy? After ten years, riders have the option to join the reserves and live on their own private estates with their dragons. They still must come in twice a year for training and take up arms again if Elantia finds itself in another war, but for the most part, their lives are their own. That leaves plenty of time for us to start businesses and invest in all sorts of ventures."

"Huh." I tapped my lower lip as I considered this. Ten years still felt like a long time, especially since I was starting later than most dragon riders, but it was still a hell of a lot better than a lifetime. "I'm guessing you'd be in the reserves if your dragon was still around."

"Indeed." A wistful look entered Tavarian's eyes for the briefest moment, then vanished. I wondered what he'd been like when his dragon was still alive—if he'd been more joyous and care-free. It was hard to imagine Tavarian soaring through the skies on dragonback, whooping and laughing like so many of the cadets did during the free portion of our flying lessons. The image of him in his silver dragon armor rose in my mind. I shivered as I remembered the cold, almost savage blaze in his eyes, the blood coating his sword.

Tavarian might not be a fan of warfare, but I had no doubt a warrior lurked beneath those perfectly pressed suits and that calm façade he wore. One who could, and had, cut down his enemies with ruthless efficiency, and possessed a will so powerful, he had even managed to survive the death of his dragon.

An impossible feat for an impossible man.

Tavarian opened his mouth to say something else, but I felt a familiar shift that could only mean one thing. "We're landing!" I exclaimed, jumping out of my chair.

"In a manner of speaking," Tavarian said as he rose from his chair. "Grab your things and come to the upper deck. We will be disembarking soon."

"Yes!" Lessie cried in my head, and I jumped. Clearly, she'd been listening. *"Does this mean I can come up too?"*

"Of course it does, silly," I said. *"I'll be right there to get you."*

But Lessie refused to wait. She was standing outside the door of my cabin, practically vibrating with excitement and impatience.

"Hurry up," she whined as I gathered up my belongings. *"I want to breathe fresh air again!"*

"If you want to hurry, then help me out here." I shoved a bag against her muzzle. *"Carry that for me, and don't shred the straps with your teeth."*

Lessie grunted, but she did as she was told, gingerly holding the bag by the straps with her mouth. While she was occupied, I strapped her saddle on so I wouldn't have to carry it, then made my way through the corridors and up the stairs, Lessie following close behind.

"Son of a hoggleswaith," I chattered, wrapping my arms around my body. I was wearing a light jacket, but it was no match for the stiff, cold winds battering the ship. "It's freezing up here!"

"That is because you are on a ship, not a dragon." Lessie pressed her warm body against me. She was right. When I'd ridden with Jallis on Kadryn, the body heat the large dragon generated had kept off the worst of the chill. *"I will keep you warm."*

"Thanks." Smiling, I patted her neck, and together we moved to stand by the bow of the ship. We were careful to stay out of the way of the crew rushing about the deck as they prepared for landing—it was a skeleton crew of only five, and they needed every spare second they could manage.

As we stood at the prow, the clouds gradually fell away, revealing a mountain range below. We seemed to be headed straight toward a valley nestled between two of the giant mountains, lush and verdant and entirely enclosed by sheer, rocky cliffs.

"This is Tavarian's secret estate?" Lessie asked. Her fiery gaze swept over the valley, which, while beautiful, appeared to be completely abandoned, with no signs of human life. *"I can hunt and roam aplenty here, but I imagine you will be quite uncomfortable."* She sounded decidedly unimpressed.

"Maybe we really are going to live in an underground bunker," I said aloud, only half-joking. Was this really the place? Maybe the crew had made a mistake.

"Over my dead body."

"We are not going to live in an underground bunker," Tavarian said in a dry voice from behind me. I jumped, then twisted around to face him—I hadn't heard him approach! "My estate wouldn't be hidden if it was easily visible from the air, would it?"

"No," I admitted, looking over my shoulder at the valley. We were halfway through our descent, low enough for the cliffs to tower around us on all sides. It would have felt like a prison if the valley wasn't so large—I estimated it to be at least six miles of fields and meadows, bordered with lushly wooded areas that butted up against the edges of the mountains. "But I make a living looking for hidden sites, and I can't see any trace of human life at all from up here." I couldn't even get a signal with my treasure sense, though that wasn't surprising. It only had a radius of about a mile, after all. "Shouldn't there be a farm, some way to raise or grow food?"

Tavarian gave me an enigmatic smile. "That would be logical, wouldn't it?"

I gnashed my teeth as he turned away, leaving me to ponder the mystery. But my annoyance quickly vanished when the ship finally touched down—even if I hadn't been glad to be back on the ground, Lessie's excitement was so palpable that it completely eclipsed my own emotions. Before I could even blink, she'd launched herself over the side of the ship and onto the ground.

"Oooh...the grass smells so good here, Zara!" she exclaimed as she rolled around in the field, wriggling like a puppy...if puppies were the size of small elephants. Her tail thrashed about, and I was glad she was a good distance from the ship, as her spikes were long enough to gouge holes in the wood. *"Come down and play with me!"*

"Hey, be careful!" I called, hurrying down the gangplank with my bag. "You've still got your saddle on!" I was thankful I hadn't strapped any of my bags onto her body—the one I'd asked her to hold was luckily discarded on the grass, but anything else on her would have been crushed.

"Oh. Right." Lessie immediately rolled onto her stomach, then craned her neck to sniff at the leather saddle perched between her shoulders. *"It has a few grass stains on it, but it should be okay with a good polish."*

"I hope Lessie is done playing," Tavarian said as he joined me. "She is going to need to help carry a few things, as we have quite a hike before we arrive at our destination."

Lessie wasn't happy about it, but she let us strap our bags to the saddle as the airship took off again, leaving us alone in the field. Thankfully, we didn't bring much—only two bags each, and I carried my pack on my back so that Lessie could do some flying. She soared overhead as Tavarian led us through the meadow, spurting little gouts of fire from her nostrils as practice. Her joy at being in the sky was infectious, and if not for Tavarian being grounded, I would have jumped onto her back and joined her up there.

"I don't blame you for wanting to fly with her," Tavarian said, reading my thoughts in that uncanny way of his. "If my dragon were here, I would vastly prefer to be up in the air with him than rooted to the ground like this."

That hint of wistfulness, of emotion, was back in his voice again, giving me the courage to ask what I had dared not the first time. "How did you lose your dragon?"

Tavarian was silent for so long that I thought he'd decided not to answer my question. "It was during the Ivory War against Zarabos. We were put in an impossible situation, and it ended badly for us."

"I'm sorry," I said, my heart aching. The thought of losing Lessie to the horrors of war, especially one as unnecessary as that one, was enough to make my blood run cold and my stomach turn to lead. "Is that why you decided to work in foreign relations after you...er...retired?"

Tavarian nodded. "It is my hope that by improving our relationships with countries across the world, both those we have made war with as well as those we've stifled in other ways, I can save dragon lives. Using these magnificent creatures"—he tilted his head up, his silver eyes briefly fixing on Lessie—"is such a waste of life, especially since dragon numbers have dwindled."

"Wouldn't you think that they would exempt Lessie from service since she's female?" I demanded. "Surely she's more valuable than most, since there are only a handful of female dragons around to reproduce."

"Her status as a female will guarantee that you are given low-risk missions and kept away from the front lines as much as possible," Tavarian said. "But no, the council will not exempt either of you from service. It is a stupid rule, but that is the way it has always been, and they are very slow to change."

The rest of the hike was spent mostly in silence as we trekked our way through the hilly forest. Despite my misgivings and homesickness, it was easy enough to get lost in the magic of this place—the colorful birds that sang as they flitted from tree to tree, the whisper of wind through the branches, the sweet, earthy smells coming from the shrubs and blossoms. My treasure sense activated automatically, and I had to resist the urge to follow the sounds coming from several valuables trying to lure me from the path.

There would be plenty of time for treasure hunting later, once we were settled.

"Ohh, I see it!" Lessie crowed about a half hour later. *"An entrance in the side of the mountain!"*

Her excitement spurred me forward, and soon enough, the tall trees gave way to a sheer cliff. A large, rectangular door was set into the wall, reminding me of tomb entrances I'd happened upon before, and I shivered a little. There was no handle I could see, but as we approached, I noticed a small depression in the door, maybe the size of a coin, with the Tavarian sigil carefully etched into it.

Tavarian fished a small bronze disc from his pocket that had a matching sigil, except this one was a relief instead of an etching. He pressed the disc against the spot in the door, and it immediately crackled with a distinct power that could only be one thing:

Magic.

"Dragon's balls," I breathed as the door immediately melted away, revealing a long corridor. Tavarian waved his hand, and the gas lamps lining the walls sprang to life, revealing deep purple carpeting and wainscoted walls.

"Welcome," Tavarian said with a grin, sweeping his arm out in dramatic fashion, "to Maravel Hall."

2

"Maravel Hall," I said. "So, we're at the western border?"

"Indeed." Tavarian spooned up a hearty bite of beef stew. "You should eat that before you pepper me with more questions. Beef stew isn't meant to be eaten cold."

I frowned, but did as he said. We sat in a tastefully appointed dining hall that would not have been out of place in a mansion. In fact, if I hadn't known we were standing inside a mountain, I would have thought we were on some upper-city tosh's estate. Tavarian had given us a full tour—the place had ten rooms, not including the staff quarters, and there were ventilation shafts and extra overhead windows cleverly hidden by vegetation to allow plenty of fresh air inside. There was also a shelter for Lessie, with a separate entrance shadowed by some giant trees where a full-grown dragon could comfortably fit. She was in there now, eating a substantial meal of mutton, while we enjoyed our lunch in here.

"I'm so glad that I made extra stew," Mrs. Barton, the house-keeper, chirped as she bustled in to refill our tankards. "I had no idea you would be arriving, and with a new dragon in tow, no less!"

"Yes, I apologize for not sending word," Tavarian said. "But we really couldn't risk it."

"That's quite all right," she said as she poured from the pitcher of ale in her hands. "We're just glad to have you back."

"It must be lonely, living here all by themselves," I said quietly as Mrs. Barton left the room. She and her husband, both in their forties, were the caretakers of this hidden estate and lived here year-round. "Do they ever get to leave?"

"They get a two-week vacation once a year," Tavarian said. "But they are quite content. They have little desire to spend much time in the outside world."

I frowned at that. Mr. Barton had been a bit taciturn when I'd met him, but Mrs. Barton had a cheerful manner about her that seemed well suited for hosting parties and socializing with fellow townsfolk. I wondered what had made them choose life under the mountain. Even a well-paid job couldn't be worth it if you couldn't enjoy the fruits of your labor but once a year.

After lunch, Tavarian quizzed me about the progress I'd made in my lessons, both with and without Lessie. He also took Lessie and me out in the field and had us run through various maneuvers to test our competence. Overall, he was impressed with Lessie's progress given that she was only a few months old, but we still had a long way to go, and he wrote out a rigorous study and training program for both of us that took nearly all our available time.

"Bank left," Tavarian ordered during one such training exercise through the magical communication device clipped to my ear.

I relayed the command, and Lessie did so, swerving back toward the center of the valley. *"I wish he would let us near the cliffsides,"* she complained to me.

"Dive ten feet, then flatten out," Tavarian said.

Lessie followed the command, though she bristled a little. *"I know how you feel,"* I said in a soothing voice even as my stomach leaped into my throat from the sudden drop, *"but Tavarian is right to be concerned. I know how strong and smart you are, but in dragon years you're still just a baby."*

"A baby wouldn't be able to carry an adult human on her back," Lessie grumbled. *"And how am I ever going to be able to make it over those cliffs if he won't let me try?"*

I glanced toward the cliffs. They were several hundred feet high, their jagged points sheltering us from the outside world, but the cliffs themselves weren't the issue. It was the steep updrafts that had battered the airship as we'd come in for our landing, updrafts that could toss a small dragon like Lessie around as if she were a ragdoll.

"We've only been here for ten days," I reminded Lessie as we flew in a small circle over the field. *"I'm sure Tavarian will let us try it in a couple of days."*

"Attack left," Tavarian ordered, and Lessie immediately dove for

the ground, her maw stretched wide open. She swooped down over a small grove of trees, miming the action of spewing fire over a group of soldiers, though of course she didn't do it in real life. Tavarian had made it very clear that we were to use no fire on the ground—the valley got plenty of rain, but it would still be all too easy to set the forests and fields ablaze.

Tavarian ordered a few more maneuvers, using the magical earpiece to give us corrections and feedback with each one. But as I thought back to the training drills at the academy, I wished Major Falkieth were here with her dragon. She and the older cadets had been able to demonstrate maneuvers for us, and had even staged mock battles so we could practice on a live opponent. It would be so much easier if there were another dragon here to show us...

"ZARA!" Lessie shrieked. *"LOOK!"*

I glanced up and would have fallen off the saddle if my feet hadn't been secured in the stirrups. A dragon, easily the size of a small house, soared straight over the cliffs, its giant wings briefly blotting out the sky. Lessie's body trembled with excitement as the other dragon tucked its wings to the sides of its body and dove for the ground, its silver scales flashing in the sunlight, heading straight toward Tavarian.

Silver scales.

"Dragon's balls," I choked out. "It can't be."

"It has to be."

Sure enough, as Lessie and I landed, the silver dragon was

nuzzling Tavarian, purring so loudly the ground vibrated beneath my feet. Tavarian was grinning, his face transformed as he stroked the dragon's enormous head, and as I stood there, a flush crept over my cheeks, like I was intruding on a private moment and should turn my face and wait for them to finish their reunion.

And yet, I couldn't look away.

Lessie, on the other hand, had no such considerations. She gave the silver dragon about ten seconds, then trotted over to him. The other dragon turned, and the two of them immediately began sniffing each other.

"So," I said, coming over to Tavarian. "Your dead dragon isn't so dead after all, is he?"

"I never said Muza was dead," Tavarian said mildly, but the devilish glint in his eyes told a different story. "I merely said that he didn't make it back. I never specified what happened to him afterward."

"So, your dragon has been living out here this entire time?" I exclaimed. "So far apart from you? Why would you willingly choose to be separated like that?"

"Because I didn't want Muza to suffer for Elantia's actions," Tavarian said quietly. He turned his gaze back to his dragon, and there was so much affection and pain in his eyes that it stole my breath. "If I'd brought him back with me to Elantia, he and I would have just been sent off to fight another war. So, I set him free instead."

I wanted to ask Tavarian more about that, but Muza turned toward me, pinning me with eyes the exact color of a tropical ocean. My breath came out of me in a whoosh as he extended his neck, nostrils flaring as he sniffed me.

"He says he likes you," Tavarian offered, "and Lessie as well."

"Oh, good." I ran a hand along his nose, admiring his silver scales. They were the exact color of Tavarian's eyes, and of the dragon armor he'd worn the night he and Lessie had rescued me from Salcombe. The dragon gave me a rumbling purr as he allowed me to pet him, then promptly turned away and nudged Tavarian's hip.

Tavarian chuckled. "Your lessons are finished," he told me. "You may take the rest of the day off."

Lessie and I looked at each other, then headed back to Maravel Hall. As much as we would have liked to stay and quiz Tavarian and Muza, we understood they needed time to reconnect after being apart for...for how long? Months? Years? Just how often did Tavarian visit his dragon? And if Muza stayed here in this valley, then why hadn't he been here when we arrived?

"Muza doesn't live here in the valley," Tavarian said later on as we feasted on a dinner of roasted boar and root vegetables. "He lives in a far-off, secret place, one that has never been discovered by any nation and never will, so long as there is breath in my body. This estate acts as a sort of go-between point for us, and we meet here once a year."

"Once a year?" I winced. "How long have you two been doing this? Ten years? Twenty?"

"Sixteen," Tavarian said. "And yes, it is incredibly difficult. Most dragon riders would not be able to withstand the mental toll such a long separation takes, but the fact that I am half-mage seems to help combat the effects."

I shook my head. Clearly, Tavarian was much stronger than I had ever given him credit for. When we'd first met, I thought he was just another pompous sky dweller like the others of his kind, or worse, another Salcombe out to take advantage of me. But the more I got to know him, the more I realized how wrong I was. Beneath the stony façade, he was intelligent, considerate, and even kind. Someone I could look up to.

Someone I could care about.

"Has there been any progress on the hunt for Salcombe?" I asked. I knew Tavarian could communicate with Captain Marcas and his fellow councilors for very brief periods using a magical device not dissimilar to the earpiece I wore during flying lessons.

Tavarian shook his head. "I would have thought he'd be caught, since there is a nationwide manhunt for him, but it seems your old mentor is annoyingly clever. It is entirely possible that by this point he has managed to slip across the border or onto a ship."

I nodded. "Salcombe is very resourceful, not to mention wealthy. I wouldn't be surprised if he'd managed to barter a spell to disguise himself or something." Ironic, really, that a mage would be helping him, considering that he was hunting for the World

Eater's heart, the very thing that the mages of old had sworn to protect.

Sighing, I picked at my food as I thought back to the last time Salcombe and I had talked. He was the reason I'd met Lord Tavarian—to settle a debt, he'd sent me to Tavarian's estate to steal a piece of the heart, and I'd ended up with Lessie instead. He'd tried to convince me Tavarian was collecting the pieces to summon the dragon god, and by the time I'd figured out the truth, it had been too late. Salcombe already had at least one piece, and he was willing to do whatever it took to get his hands on the rest of them.

Including sacrificing my life.

My nose ached with phantom pain as I remembered his fist plowing into my face. The ugly, twisted look of rage and zeal had been more sickening than the strike itself. I'd never deluded myself into thinking Salcombe was a good man—he'd taken me in and raised me, but he'd also used me to find treasure and steal it for him when the item he wanted was already in someone else's hands. Back when I was a young teenager, when stealing was as natural as breathing and I was starved for affection, starved for any scrap of home and hearth I could get, I didn't care that Salcombe was using me. I'd been too blind and naïve to see it.

But I wasn't that naïve little girl anymore. I knew that family and friendship wasn't about what someone else could do for you. It was about what the two of you could do *together*. About the memories you could make, the challenges you could tackle, the feats you could accomplish. It was about climbing the mountain together, not cutting someone else's rope so you could get to the top first.

Salcombe had never understood that. But I had the feeling that Lord Tavarian did.

The next couple of weeks passed markedly different than the first. Muza's presence changed everything—Lessie was more eager than ever to prove herself, while Tavarian was a little more laid back and indulgent. He still wouldn't let Lessie anywhere near the cliffs—and neither would Muza, for that matter—but we did start practicing some more exciting maneuvers, like barrel rolls and corkscrews. Lessie and I even got to practice fire-bombing dummies in a fire-proofed clearing, an activity she absolutely delighted in.

He also made me drill rigorously with the crossbow, both on and off Lessie's back. I hated these exercises the most, especially when he made me try to shoot game from hundreds of feet in the air. But I couldn't solely rely on Lessie's brawn and firepower when I was in the air, and the crossbow was one of the best weapons I could use while in the sky.

"I wish Muza could come back with us to Elantia," Lessie said plaintively as I groomed her one night. *"It seems so sad to me that when we're finished, he'll have to go back in hiding again."*

"I agree," I said as I stroked a cloth over her scales. The cloth was soaked with a special, slightly spicy herbal solution that cut through grime and strengthened scales. "But on the other hand, this is the most time Muza has spent with his rider in years. I have no doubt these new memories he's making with us will last him for a good, long while."

"Or make his pain that much harder to bear," Lessie argued. *"I am starting to think you are right about these wars, Zara. I do want to smite our enemies, but not at the expense of my fellow dragons. Muza said that if I ever were to tire of Elantia or get fed up being commanded by people who don't have my best interests at heart, to come and stay with him. He tells me that the place he lives in is beautiful and that I would feel right at home."*

"Is that so?" I asked, a little taken aback. I'd never thought about it, but what if Lessie decided she didn't want to be with me anymore? That she would prefer to go off and live on her own, with someone of her own kind—

"Don't be silly," Lessie said, her voice gentling. She craned her neck over her shoulder and nuzzled my cheek. *"While I do intend to visit Muza's island someday, I would never abandon you. We are bound together both in this life and the next."*

Smiling, I nuzzled her back. "Do you really think there's a next life, or an afterlife?" I asked. The ancient Elantians had certainly thought so, before the dragon god had come to our world and shattered our faith, and there were still other countries around the world, that worshipped various deities.

"Of course there is," Lessie said. *"Our souls burn too hot and too bright to be snuffed out by one mere lifetime. Our bodies may break down, but we continue on."*

The conviction in her voice was so firm, so powerful, that I nearly believed it.

3

"I never thought reading could be boring," I said when I came into the dining area for lunch, "but this textbook is so dry, I should try reading it before bedtime. It would put me to sleep instantly."

Tavarian raised his eyebrows as I dumped the heavy black book on the table, right next to a bowl full of salad. "That textbook is a classic," he said mildly. "I believe my great-grandfather was the one who added it to my family library. You should be more careful with it."

"Did he buy it to use as a doorstop?" I asked crossly as I forked salad onto my plate. Tavarian gave me a look, and I grudgingly nudged the book a few more inches away, safely out of range. "Really, Tavarian, I already know most of the history surrounding these battles. I have no plans to be an officer, and the actual drills and exercises we do should be more than sufficient to help me through my military service. I don't need a blow-by-blow account of every single battle in Elantia's illustrious war career."

"Be sure to tell the examiners that when you go back to the academy for testing," Tavarian said, his voice even drier than the despised textbook. "I'm sure they'll be very understanding."

I was about to fire back with a brilliant retort when a sharp pain sliced into my...wing? I cried out, jerking in my chair, terror ballooning inside me so fast and hard I could barely breathe. My heart was pounding, my face covered in sweat—

"Zara!" Tavarian was next to me, gripping my face in his hands. "Zara, snap out of it! It's not yours!"

His words were like an anchor, and I latched onto them, focusing on the deep silver of his irises to pull myself back. *Not yours,* I told myself, trying to separate from Lessie's feelings. I managed to pull away from her agony, reducing it from a sharp stab to a dull throb.

"Lessie?" I called out to her, my heart still pounding frantically. *"Lessie, what happened?"*

"I tore my wing," she wailed. *"On a tree branch!"*

"Shit." I batted Tavarian's hands away from me. "We have to go get her."

"Muza tells me the injury is not life-threatening," Tavarian said calmly. "They are three miles away—at that distance, it would be better to wait for Muza to bring her back."

"Can he do that?" I asked. Muza was much larger than Lessie, but she was no hatchling anymore.

"He is strong enough to manage the distance."

The two of us waited outside the entrance to the dragon stable, and sure enough, Muza arrived a few minutes later with a bedraggled Lessie in tow, gently held in his clutches. She whined pitifully as he deposited her on the ground, and sure enough, her left wing dangled limply, a bloody tear the size of my arm in the upper part of the membrane.

"Oh, you poor thing," I crooned aloud, wrapping my arms around her neck. "What happened?"

But Lessie only buried her face in my neck, refusing to say a word. From the intense embarrassment I felt through our bond, I imagined that she'd done something foolish and was too ashamed to relive the incident.

"Muza?" I asked the silver dragon.

"He says that they were hunting trozla on the eastern side of the valley," Tavarian answered, referring to the graceful, four-legged animals with long necks, antlers, and purplish-grey fur that liked to roam these areas. "Lessie decided to go for a larger specimen, but she misjudged the descent and tore her wing on a tree branch. She was, ah, showing off a bit."

"I really thought I could do it," Lessie sniffled. *"I'm so stupid, and I've made a fool of myself in front of Muza!"*

"Oh stop," I said, stroking the side of her neck as I switched to mental speech. *"Muza isn't going to think less of you just because you*

made a mistake. You're still a dragonling, Lessie. Making mistakes is part of growing up, part of learning. You can't be perfect all the time."

She gave a deep sigh. *"I've spent hundreds of years dreaming of this moment,"* she said. *"Of flying through the air with my kind and impressing the others with my speed and agility and hunting prowess. I suppose I became so good at it in my dreams that it didn't occur to me that reality wouldn't be as effortless as I thought."*

I smiled. *"Believe me, everyone goes through this. I'm sure if you asked Muza, he'd tell you that he's seen dozens of baby dragons make mistakes or hurt themselves while learning how to fly. He's probably done it himself."*

She was silent for a long moment. *"He says that when he was two years old, he was play-wrestling in the sky with another dragon and accidentally fell into a tree. He had dozens of cuts on his wings and broke two bones. It took two weeks to heal,"* she added smugly.

I laughed, feeling most of her embarrassment fade away. "See?" I said aloud, patting her neck. "This isn't so bad. You'll only need a few days."

"Let's get her to the stables," Tavarian suggested. "I might be able to reduce that time a bit."

"You can?" I blinked. "How?"

But Tavarian was already moving inside, his dragon following after him. Sighing, I led Lessie into the stable, which was really just a large, circular room with cushy hay piles for the dragons to sit on. There weren't even food or watering troughs, since the dragons hunted daily for their food and they drank from a small pond not far away.

I guided Lessie toward her hay pile, supporting her wing so it wouldn't drag as she walked. Tavarian had left the room, but he came back shortly with a bucket of water, a small bottle containing a pungent poultice, and a few rags.

"Here," he said, handing them to me. "Let's get that wound clean."

I did as he said, using the water and rag to dab the blood away. Lessie hissed the first time I touched the wound, but gradually she relaxed, and I was able to get it all clean.

"Good." Tavarian gestured for me to move aside, then he knelt in the hay next to Lessie. He dabbed some of the poultice into the wound, and Lessie moaned pitifully. "To prevent infection," he explained, then laid his thumb directly on top of the gash, at the end farthest from him.

I gasped as energy crackled from his hand, and Lessie yelped. But it was more from the surprise than the pain, and I watched in astonishment as Tavarian sealed the wound inch by inch, moving his thumb across the gash until all that was left was a raised scar.

"She'll need a day or two to heal completely," Tavarian said when it was done, "but this should get her back into the air much quicker."

I frowned, remembering the mage who had healed my broken

rib. He'd completed the procedure in less than ten minutes. "You're not trained," I realized.

Tavarian gave me a wry smile. "I am self-taught out of necessity," he said. "Ideally, I would have been able to apprentice under a mage, but my mother only carried the bloodline—she had no magic herself, and while she was able to teach me exercises to get control of my abilities, she could not teach me the art, and had no surviving relatives. Going to a master would have risked exposing myself, so I tried to learn as much as I could through the magic texts I was able to get my hands on. Unfortunately, textbook learning can only get you so far when it comes to magic. There are many things I do not know."

"I wonder how many others are like you out there," I mused aloud. "Mages who don't have family or friends to teach them to use their abilities."

"There are secret communities where mages come together and pool their resources to learn from one another," Tavarian said. "There is at least one in Zuar City. But there is a rigorous screening process to get in, and there was no way to apply without revealing myself."

I pursed my lips. "Surely you could bribe some mage into teaching you," I said. "Can't you use a blood oath to make sure they don't tell anyone else, as you did to me?"

He smiled. "I could try that, but by all accounts, mages are tricky folk. I don't know enough about magic to feel confident about using it to bind someone who is far more practiced than me. They could just as easily figure out a way to twist the magic around on me or use a loophole of some kind that I did not foresee."

I thought about that as I got ready for bed that night, tying my long, curly red hair into a pineapple bun so it wouldn't look like a total nightmare the next morning. It seemed like Tavarian and I had something in common—both of us had one foot in the dragon rider world, and another foot in a world that didn't quite fit with the first one. I wondered if that was one of the reasons he'd treated me with kindness, if perhaps it wasn't just his investment in Lessie that spurred him to look out for my well-being.

Why does it have to be any of those things? a voice in my head argued. *Can't it just be that Tavarian decided to look out for you because he has a conscience? You help others all the time, Zara, with no thought for yourself. Isn't it possible someone might do that for you?*

But that wasn't my experience. I'd had few friends I could rely on in my life—Carina was one of them, but she was usually too busy wrangling her feckless brother, Brolian, to be a good shoulder to lean on. I'd learned about human nature at Salcombe's knee—that everyone was out for themselves, and you should never help someone unless there was a good chance you would benefit in some way, because when the time came to return the favor, there was always a risk that the person you'd helped wouldn't be able to deliver.

I'd taken great pleasure in breaking all those rules. Because the truth was, even though Salcombe's philosophy ensured he was wealthy and secure, it also cut him off from society. I didn't want to be like him, holed up in his mansion with only his books and treasures for company. I wanted to live, to be surrounded by people I cared about, to laugh and dance and savor everything this world had on offer.

And I couldn't do that if I built an iron cage around my heart, as Salcombe had. A heart that was now so withered and twisted, so disconnected from humanity, he was willing to sacrifice the entire world for the sake of power.

The next afternoon, I half-expected Tavarian to let me ride Muza instead of Lessie, since she was still healing. Instead, he called me to the training room, which I'd only used a handful of times since arriving.

I walked into the room dressed in comfortable training clothes, expecting Tavarian to spend the hour running me through various self-defense techniques and weapons drills. But when I walked in and saw him standing in the center of the training ring wearing nothing but a pair of loose trousers, I stumbled over the threshold and nearly planted my face into the ground.

"Miss Kenrook?" Tavarian spun around to face me, his brow furrowed in concern. He'd been studying the weapons mounted on the wall when I walked in, giving me a view of his very well-muscled back, but his front was even better. Pale skin poured over a broad chest and trim waist, every single dip and ridge of muscle on display. I'd seen my fair share of naked men before, but most of the guys I'd slept with were on the bulky side. Tavarian, however, was lean, his compact build designed to house his sheer power and masculinity as efficiently as possible. And he wasn't just well built—he was practically a work of art, perfectly proportioned. The only interruption across that smooth expanse of skin was the trail of black hair that went from his belly button and disappeared beneath the waistband of his trousers. It might as well have been a flaming red arrow that said, "THIS WAY TO PARADISE."

"Sorry." I picked myself up off the ground, my cheeks warm, and cleared my throat. "I didn't realize we were training half-naked today. Do I need to take my shirt off too?"

I expected Tavarian to show some measure of humility, but he only smirked. "If that makes you more comfortable."

Dammit. My face felt like it was wreathed in flames. I wasn't used to someone turning my snarky comments on me like that, especially not a guy like Tavarian. And since I damn well couldn't admit it would *not*, in fact, make me more comfortable if I took my shirt off, I folded my arms and said nothing.

"Now," Tavarian said, business-like. "You've spent a great deal of time on academics and flying lessons because those are the two areas you need most catching up on based on the testing we've done. However, it is important that we practice combat training, as it is not at all unusual for a dragon rider to be unseated during warfare. The last thing your dragon needs is for you to get skewered on an enemy's sword because you could not defend yourself properly."

I nodded, remembering the brief battle Lessie and I had engaged in on Salcombe's secondary estate. I'd jumped from her back to tackle and kill one of the guards while Lessie had gone after the other. I was already fairly well-trained in combat thanks to Salcombe's tutors, but I wasn't a master by any means, even though I'd trained at the academy as well. If something had gone wrong, if one of those men had killed me before I'd killed them, Lessie would have been dead.

"Okay," I said, glancing toward the weapons rack. "So, what are we training with, then? Can we practice with my dragon blade?" I flipped open the sheath hanging from the belt on my waist and pulled out the double-bladed knife.

Tavarian's silver eyes gleamed as I spun the weapon in my hand, extending the blades to six inches on either side with a mere thought. Jallis had told me the weapon was tied to my bloodline when he'd given it to me, and that was why I was able to control it. I knew it was a clue to my heritage, but since the sigil that had once been affixed to the handle was long gone, I had no idea which house it belonged to.

"No," he said. "We won't be using weapons at all today."

"Hand to hand, then?" I brightened right up at that. I was pretty handy with my daggers, and the dragon blade seemed to come naturally to me, but most other weapons were hit-and-miss. Empty-handed combat, on the other hand, was right up my alley.

"Yes." Tavarian assumed a boxer's stance, his feet level and his hands close by his head. "Your task for today is simple—try to hit me."

"My pleasure."

I assumed a stance of my own, a little more fluid—hands out in front of me to strike and parry, front foot pointed at him, back foot angled a little to the side. Part of me wanted to jump in, to strike hard and fast, but I knew Tavarian expected that. So instead I threw a few test jabs, trying to gauge his rhythm. He parried each one with a small flick of his wrist, barely moving at all.

"I said try to *hit* me, not *tap* me," Tavarian said, a hint of impatience in his voice. "Is this what you normally try to do when an opponent is trying to hurt you?"

"No," I said, and brought my back foot up, lightning-quick, in a crescent kick. Tavarian blocked, and I pivoted to the side, snapping out my leg once more. He jumped back with a mere millimeter of space between us, then grabbed my leg and yanked it out from under me.

"Hey!" I cried as I fell. I would have landed on my back, maybe even my head, but Tavarian yanked me flush against him, his pelvis meshing right up against my inner thigh.

"Don't ever leave your leg out like that again," he said, eyes flashing. He released me before I could react, and I stumbled backward. "Your retractions must be as fast as your strikes."

Rather than wasting my breath on a reply, I struck again, this time for the ribs. Tavarian blocked with his elbow. I unleashed a flurry of punches and kicks, aiming for the face, the abdomen, the kidneys, but nothing landed. Even more infuriating, he was parrying and dodging with minimal effort, using the most miniscule motions to evade my blows. He was ridiculously fast, his footwork far superior to anyone I'd ever fought before.

Well then, I thought, *I'll just have to take his footwork out of the equation.*

I feinted left to distract him, then dropped to the ground and kicked my leg out. Tavarian went down in an instant, but before I could gloat, he hooked one foot around the back of my ankle and the other one in front. The next thing I knew I was on top of him, then beneath him, his hard frame pressing me into the ground.

"Very good," he said, his breath warm on my face. His nose was barely an inch from mine, and I could feel every ridge of muscle through the thin cotton top I wore. "I told you to hit me, not take me down, but I'll give you credit for ingenuity anyway. However," he said, clamping his thighs around my hips tight enough to make me squirm, "if you are going to take someone down, you must be prepared to either finish him off or run away. Staying within striking range was a big mistake."

Tavarian spent the rest of the lesson adjusting what he called my "bad habits"—forcing me into tighter stances and using controlled motions to parry and evade. The new style he was teaching me went against years of training and made me grit my teeth—but he had a point. The sweeping motions and wider stances were pretty and graceful, but I'd never used them outside of sparring. On the streets, faced with someone who was trying to rob or rape or kill you, the best course of action was to get out of there as fast as possible. My instructor had always told me running was the best option, and my agility had usually been enough to get me out of most situations without having to engage. Anything else was quickly solved with a dagger or a smoke bomb.

But as I'd learned recently, I wouldn't always have my bag of tricks or my weapons on me. And relying on my dragon to swoop in wasn't a solution—not when my failure to defend myself could mean death for both of us.

4

"*Z*ara," Lessie called. *"There's an airship landing in the field!"*

My head snapped up from the book I'd been studying, and I jumped out of my chair. It had been over a month since Lessie and I had come to this secret vale, and this was the first time we'd had any visitors since Muza.

"Coming!" I called back, rushing out of my room and down the hall. I burst out of the hidden door to see Lessie waiting impatiently for me, her saddle and harness waiting on the ground next to her. I quickly strapped them on, then jumped on her back.

Lessie barely waited for me to settle on her back before she took off, heading for the meadow where the airship had first dropped us off. It only took us a minute to get there, and we landed the same time it did. Tavarian already waited in the field, along with Mr. and Mrs. Barton, though his own dragon was conspicuously absent. I had a feeling that, aside from the caretakers, Lessie and

I were the only ones that knew of Muza's existence, and Tavarian wanted to keep it that way.

"Ah, there you are," Tavarian said. "Lessie can help us bring these back." He gestured to the large supply crates being wheeled off the ship. It occurred to me that the Bartons usually received shipments on their own, and the rope sled standing behind them confirmed my suspicion. Did they typically carry that all the way back by themselves?

Lessie huffed. *"I am not tying myself to that thing,"* she said. *"I am too small to make it through the forest anyway. I will hold the crates and fly them back one by one."*

Tavarian nodded when I relayed the message. "I already surmised as much," he said. "Though we will still transport some of these on the sled."

"Ah, there you are, Miss Kenrook!" one of the crew members called. He shoved a twine-wrapped package into my hands. "There are some letters in there for you."

"There are?" My skin prickled in excitement as I turned the package over in my hand. Had Carina and Rhia written to me? What about Jallis?

In the end, we loaded up three of the crates onto the sled, and Lessie agreed to take three more herself. The trek back to the mountain residence wasn't too bad—Tavarian used his magic to lighten the load a bit, and between the four of us, we got the sled back without much effort.

The moment we were inside, I rushed into the dining area and tossed the package on the table. I tore it open and immediately sorted through it, tossing anything that wasn't mine in a pile at the head of the table. A lot of it was official correspondence for Tavarian, but there were a few letters from my friends, and also some periodicals detailing the latest and greatest from Elantia as well as a few other countries. I set the Elantian paper aside and gave the rest to Tavarian to look over.

Dear Zara, Jallis's letter read, his bold, masculine script flowing across the cream-colored paper. *I hope you and Lessie are thriving under Lord Tavarian's care and tutelage. Despite what I said to you about him when we first met, he is an honorable man and a good rider. By the time you come back, I won't be surprised if you and Lessie end up flying circles around Kadryn and me. Don't stay away too long, though—I miss you, and I can't wait until you're back so we can go on more adventures together.*

Yours, Jallis.

I grinned like a schoolgirl and put the letter aside to read Carina's next. I'd respond to them once I finished reading them all. There was no rush anyway—the airship had to go on to another town to fuel up and would pass by in a day or two to pick up return mail before heading back to Elantia.

Hey Zara, Carina wrote in the sparse but elegant hand that covered our ledgers. *I hope you and Lessie are okay, and that you're not going stir-crazy being shut away wherever Tavarian's hidden you. I wish you'd been able to tell us where you've gone, but as long as my letters reach you, I guess I can live without knowing. After all, I'm a wimp. If someone tried to torture your location out of me, I would be singing in five seconds flat. I still love you, though. Please don't burn this letter.*

I laughed, shaking my head, then continued reading.

Things are going well at the shop, but the two guards Captain Marcas have stationed here are a nuisance. They follow me everywhere, and I think they scare off some of the customers because they are so intimidating. But I guess that's better than getting kidnapped by Salcombe. I just wish they'd find him, but there's no sign, even though they've practically torn the city apart.

Come home soon, Zara. The Treasure Trove just isn't the same without you.

Love, Carina.

I blinked tears out of my eyes and gingerly put the letter aside before I accidentally ruined it. I missed the Treasure Trove and Carina, missed the old days where my most pressing concerns were keeping the shop running and deciding which treasures to track down next. It was true that my new life had solved most of my problems—the shop was booming, and many of my old orphan friends were employed—but being a dragon rider had also brought along a host of new ones.

The more power and wealth you have, the more people will show up at your doorstep trying to wrench a piece of the pie from you. Salcombe's words echoed in my head, and I shoved them aside with a low growl. I didn't need any more of his advice, thank you very much.

I opened Rhia's letter next, hoping her words would cheer me up.

Dear Zara, she wrote, her flowery script dancing across the page. *I'd ask if you are well, but I have no doubt you and Lessie are doing just fine. The two of you have such fire in your souls that I doubt even a hailstorm could keep you down. I can't wait for you to come back and show everyone what you've learned from Lord Tavarian.*

I smirked, wondering if I should write back and tell her that I got up close and personal with his abs today. Not that I thought there was any potential there, but the look on Rhia's face would be absolutely priceless.

A look that you won't be able to see, I reminded myself.

Things are going well here, Rhia continued. *Aria is back, but after the stunt she pulled on you, most of her old clique won't associate with her. There's a lot less tension overall, and I've even made a few more friends with some of the girls from the older houses. I think your time here has shown them that class distinction doesn't matter as much as they thought it did.*

I blinked in surprise at that. I knew I'd shaken things up during my time at the academy, but I hadn't thought I'd made *that* much of a difference. The idea that I'd changed a few opinions, opened a few minds, gave me a warm, fuzzy feeling. But was it too good to be true? After all, these girls would be thrown into the Elantian army as soon as they were finished with their training and molded into whatever the military needed them to be.

And so will I.

I shook off the thought and kept reading.

Unfortunately, the academy's atmosphere has started to get tense again. There are rumors we are headed off to war again, and that the older cadets will be drafted. Ykos and I are probably too young to be called, but Jallis and the other riders of his age will be summoned if his father can't resolve things peacefully with Zallabar.

I miss you, Zara, but I'm glad that you are far away from all this. Don't come back too soon.

Rhia.

I set the letter on the table, my stomach churning. War with Zallabar? But I thought Tavarian had managed to calm things down. What changed? Had we done something to provoke them again? Anxiety brewed in my chest, making me antsy. What if Jallis and Rhia did get called off to war, while I was stuck here in this valley? Would I come back to find out my friends were dead, their bodies torn apart by cannon fire?

I snatched up the Elantian paper, hoping to find answers. Poring through the articles, I quickly discovered that in the past two weeks, a General Richstein had taken over the Zallabarian government in a bloody coup. Evidently, he'd wanted to go to war with Elantia for years, and this latest change in plans from the current ruler had tipped him over the edge. My heart sank as I kept reading—apparently Richstein promised the Zallabarian citizens riches beyond their wildest dreams once they successfully conquered Elantia and took their revenge for past humiliations they'd suffered at our hands.

"Miss Kenrook?" Tavarian's voice jerked me out of the article, and I looked up. He stood at the head of the table, looking at me with concern. "Is everything all right? You look as if you've seen a ghost."

"Here." I shoved the paper at him. "Read this article."

Tavarian's silver eyes darted across the page. His expression went from mild concern to unpleasant surprise. By the time he'd finished reading, his eyes were simmering with frustration.

"It would seem our efforts at peace have been sabotaged," he said, sitting down in the chair. "I have met General Richstein before—he is a madman who cannot be reasoned with. If he has declared his intentions, it is only a matter of time before he acts on them."

I wanted to ask Tavarian more about the conflict, but he held up a hand, and instead attacked the pile of correspondence on his desk. Each letter he read seemed to groove more lines of worry into his brow, and by the time he was finished, his face was a hard mask.

"This is worse than I'd feared," he said, putting the last letter aside. "According to our intelligence department, the Zallabarian government has been mobilizing their forces and offering alliances to other countries that Elantia has offended in the past. There are quite a number of those, but thankfully most are still too small to risk involvement, even if they have a larger country like Zallabar on their side."

"But some *are* interested," I said, reading between the lines.

"Indeed, Traggar and Quoronis are in talks with Zallabar as we speak."

My blood went cold. Traggar was a country of blond, pale-skinned brutes who lived on a series of islands to the west, while Quoronis, a nation of passionate, dark-haired people, lived to the south of us. With Zallabar to the east, we were hemmed in on three sides.

"We have to do something about this," I said. My palms grew clammy at the thought of going to war with three countries. If all of them decided to attack at the same time, we were doomed, dragons or not. "I know how this is going to end—with our government sending out every single rider and able-bodied soldier to fight, even those of us whose dragons are still babies." My blood sizzled at the thought of Lessie being thrown into battle only to be cut down before her life had even started.

"I know that," Tavarian said tersely. He drummed his long fingers on the tabletop, his lips pursed as he thought. "I have a decent relationship with the Foreign Minister of Quoronis, and some political leverage there for favors exchanged in the past. If I can neutralize them, our chances of survival will increase exponentially."

"Then we'll have to go there," I said. "When do we leave?"

"*We* are not leaving," Tavarian said grimly. "*I* am. You and Lessie will stay here, where it is safe, and continue your studies and training as best as you can until I get back."

"No way!" I slapped my hand on the table, indignant. "I'm not a child you can just leave behind, Tavarian. I've been to Quoronis plenty of times, and I know their culture well. Let me come along. Maybe I can help somehow."

"Even if you could help somehow, you would have to leave Lessie behind," Tavarian said. "She is too inexperienced a flier to keep up with Muza and me, and I'm not sure she can even clear the cliffs yet. You know how important it is that I get to Quoronis post-haste."

"You're not going to take an airship?" I scowled. I'd thought that Muza would stay behind with Lessie, but now that I knew he wasn't, Tavarian had a point. I couldn't leave Lessie here all by herself for days or even weeks on end. It wasn't right, and I knew she wouldn't do that to me.

"No, Muza will be faster, especially as he will not have to make refueling stops along the way," Tavarian said. "I've managed to perfect a sort of shielding spell, so he can drop me off without being seen before returning to his own home. I will return here by airship when I am finished."

"Fine," I grumbled. I didn't like the idea of being stuck here in this valley, but I couldn't risk Tavarian's mission just because of my selfish desires. While I was decent at negotiating with traders and salesmen, politics and warfare were another matter entirely. Tavarian would be able to work better if he didn't have to worry about me, and he'd already wasted weeks training me while the country slid deeper and deeper into peril.

The two of them left that night, and Lessie and I stood outside, watching as they disappeared into the darkness. *I don't understand why Muza couldn't just come back here after dropping Tavarian off,"* Lessie said forlornly. *"He says he was supposed to return home for a week anyway, so he could attend to other matters, but what sort of obligations does a free dragon have?"*

"You've got me," I said, petting her flank. I wondered if maybe there was more to this secret place of Muza's than he or Tavarian had let on, but I doubted I would find out anytime soon. I wasn't going to push, either—the fact that Tavarian had trusted Lessie and me with Muza's secret was an honor. Even if I was bound to silence, Lessie wasn't, and she could tell the other dragons about Muza when we returned home. She wouldn't, of course, but Tavarian didn't know that for sure. Lessie was a young dragon, after all.

Lessie was so forlorn about Muza's absence that I stayed with her in the stables until she fell asleep. The warmth of her body lulled me into falling asleep as well, and I woke up the next morning with a crick in my neck.

"Hey, sleepyhead," I said, nudging her big head. She let out a rumble, and I chuckled when she buried her face into the hay —the equivalent of putting a pillow over her head. I decided to let her be, so I walked out into the morning sunshine and stretched my arms over my head. I had a feeling Lessie was going through another growth spurt and needed the extra sleep.

The smell of grass and earth and flowering trees lulled me deeper into the forest, and I decided to go for a walk to clear my head and stretch my muscles. I wasn't ready to go back to the Hall—I already knew I would feel Tavarian's absence the moment I stepped inside. He and Muza had become part of our lives these past few weeks, and I'd taken their companionship for granted.

Maybe I'll spend the day exploring, I told myself. After all, Tavarian wasn't around to tell me what to do. Who said I had to spend the whole time training? It had been a good while since I'd last exercised my treasure hunting abilities, and there were bound to be a few items hanging around a place like this.

I closed my eyes and activated my treasure sense, spreading it as far as it could go in the hopes that I could pick up something. I immediately picked up on something about half a mile away. Using the trick Tavarian had taught me, I called up an image of it.

"A stone statue," I muttered, focusing. "Three feet tall. Pre-Plague, maybe?"

"Good," a familiar voice said from behind me, smug and sinister all at once. "I'm glad to see your senses are still sharp. You're going to need them."

I spun around, reaching for the weapon at my hip, but it wasn't there. A blinding flash of light hit me straight in the face, and I was plunged into a deep, black darkness.

5

The repetitive sound of a whirring propeller jabbed at my consciousness, reluctantly dragging me from sleep. Keeping my eyes closed, I reached out with my other senses, trying to get an idea of where I was. The air around me was cold, and I could hear someone breathing. My clothes were still on, and there was a cushion underneath me, like the kind on a bench seat.

"How long will it take to reach Jedburgh?" Salcombe's voice was faint, as if it came from the other end of a long room, but clear as day.

"Another day, sir," a male voice answered. "But we should be able to do it with only one stop for fuel."

"Good," Salcombe said. "The fewer stops, the better, now that we have the girl on board."

The girl. A spurt of anger filled me, and I resisted the urge to fist my hands at my sides. I'd spent half my life as the closest thing he had to a daughter, and in the span of a few short months, I'd been reduced to "the girl." If I wasn't pretending to be asleep, I would have taken the nearest object and chucked it at his rotten head.

But I forced myself to push my anger aside and focus on the words. *Jedburgh.* Wracking my muddled brain, I remembered it was a small town in western Zallabar. *Dragon's balls.* We were headed into enemy territory?

I reached out to Lessie through the bond, hoping we were still within range. To my relief, I could sense her, though her presence was faint.

"Zara?" Lessie's frantic voice burst into my mind. *"Zara, what happened? Where ARE you? I woke up and you were GONE!"*

"It's Salcombe," I told her, trying not to let her panic rile me up. But the hairs on my arms stood up on end, and my skin prickled. *"He and his men must have snuck into the valley overnight, after Tavarian left. They jumped me while I was taking a walk in the woods. I think they used a spell to knock me out before I could call for help."*

Lessie let out a string of curses so foul, they would have been amusing if not for my current predicament. *"I'm going to kill him,"* she fumed. *"The next time I get a clear shot at him, the old bastard is mine."*

"Don't do anything crazy," I warned, a little alarmed at the fury roiling in her. I wasn't surprised that Lessie was angry, but she was seeing red, the type of rage that eroded common sense. *"Sal-*

combe has me in an airship, I think. He seems to be taking me to Zallabar, though I don't know why."

"Are you done speaking to your dragon yet?"

My eyes flew open at Salcombe's cool voice. He was sitting on the bench seat across from me with a cup of tea in his hand, looking as calm and composed as if we were sitting in his garden. I glared at him, and the corners of his mouth curled into a distinctive smirk.

"Your breathing changed," he said as I pushed myself into a sitting position. "And there are goosebumps on your arms. You've been awake for the past five minutes."

"I'm amazed you haven't bound and gagged me," I muttered, rubbing my aforementioned arms to ward off the chill I felt. While the man sitting in front of me was more like the Salcombe I knew growing up, the madman who'd punched me in the nose lurked beneath the surface. Had Salcombe's wasting illness driven him to the breaking point, or was it the World Eater himself whispering tainted promises in his ear?

Salcombe shrugged. "And why should I? You're no threat to me." He flexed his hand, shattering the teacup he held. Blood and tea dribbled down his arm as bits of china rained to the floor, and a hulking man dressed in black with knives strapped all over his body immediately sprang into action, grabbing a rag to clean up the mess.

"Are you crazy?" I shouted, then gaped as the half-dozen cuts in his palm vanished. "What...how...?"

"The dragon god's heart gives me power," Salcombe said smugly. "And this is only from a single piece. Can you imagine what I could do with all five?"

"You mean aside from raining death and destruction upon the entire world?" I said, glaring at him. At the same time, I opened up my treasure sense, searching for the piece of heart. To my surprise, it wasn't anywhere near the airship.

"Oh, Zara." Salcombe heaved a sigh of disappointment. "Your lack of imagination has always been your greatest weakness. Zakyiar isn't going to destroy the entire world. In fact, the two of us have grand plans for it. And you could be a part of them, if you weren't so stubborn."

"I'm flattered," I said, crossing my arms. "Now can you please tell me what the hell you want, so I can refuse?"

Salcombe curled his lip. "It's a pity I never managed to cure you of your flippant attitude. But I suppose that's what I get for taking in a street rat. As far as what I want," he said before I could snarl at him, "you already know I'm after the other pieces of the heart. And unless you want you and your dragon to die, you are going to help me find them."

I pinched the bridge of my nose. *This again.* "Salcombe, threatening Lessie's and my lives isn't much of an incentive when your endgame is to bring back a dragon god that literally devours worlds. You're basically giving me a choice between dying now or dying later."

Salcombe's eyes glittered. "While I would be the first to admit you do not deserve a second chance, I cannot refute the logic in your words. Very well, if you need an incentive, I shall give you one. Help me find the rest of the pieces, and I will ensure that you and Lessie survive the coming fallout. If you prove your loyalty now, I will ensure that you have a place by Zakyiar's side. Betray me, and when I finally resurrect him, I will ensure that you and Lessie become his playthings for a very, very long time."

I shuddered at that. I didn't know what it meant to become the plaything of a blood-thirsty, amoral dragon god, but I was confident I didn't want to find out. "Fine," I lied. "I'll help you." I might as well play along while I figured out what to do. Maybe I could find an escape window while we were traveling. It would certainly be better than allowing myself to be tortured and killed.

"By the way," Salcombe said in a silky voice, "if you are thinking about trying to find a way to escape, don't bother." He reached into his pocket and pulled out a lock of red hair. "I took a few clippings from you the first time I kidnapped you and purchased a spell from a mage to trace you through your hair."

My stomach dropped. "Is that how you managed to find me in the valley?"

"Indeed." He gave me a smile that was pure malice. "So long as I have these locks of hair, I can find you anywhere, Zara. And the next time I have to come and collect you, I won't be nearly so nice."

Salcombe returned the lock of hair to his pocket, and it took everything I had not to lunge across the space and strangle him. But the hulking brute who seemed to be part mercenary, part manservant watched me with a hungry stare, as if he would like nothing better than an excuse to put his meaty hands on me.

No thanks, I thought, returning his stare with a cool one of my own. He gave me a wolfish grin that sent icy shivers up my spine, and it took everything I had not to immediately look away. Damn. If only I had my weapons with me, or even my supply belt!

Salcombe spent the rest of the trip forcing me to be his research assistant as he combed through several texts on mage genealogy. According to him, these books contained clues to the location of another piece of heart belonging to a mage family that had relocated numerous times over the last three hundred years. Part of me wanted to set the books on fire, but the other part was reluctantly fascinated, and I was glad Salcombe was including me. Perhaps I could find some clue that would give me an advantage and use it to steer him away from the heart.

"Yes," Salcombe finally said, tapping at one of the entries in the journal he was studying. "I am convinced that Jedburgh is the last location where the Starkold family descendants lived. They owned several properties in Western Zallabar, but this is where they were when the parents died."

"It's a sad story," I said quietly. The parents had passed away from scarlet fever, leaving behind two offspring that were adopted by a relative from their mother's side. "I wonder where the children are now."

Salcombe snorted. "I don't know why you are wasting your pity on them," he said. "They had family to take them in, which is more than you had at their age."

"Gee, thanks."

Salcombe ignored my snark. "We will start with Jedburgh, but the plan is to tour all four properties," he said. "Trolbos will accompany us"—he gestured to the brute standing nearby—"as our manservant, and you will be my young wife."

"Eww." I wrinkled my nose, my skin crawling at the idea of posing as Salcombe's wife. Did that mean I had to let him paw me?

"Don't worry," Salcombe said dryly. "I will behave as if I am the pinnacle of propriety. I have no interest in a flighty, naïve woman young enough to be my daughter."

I should have been relieved, but my stomach was a knotted mess of nerves over this entire situation. "You do realize we are on the brink of war with Zallabar, right?" I pressed. "What if they decide to take us prisoner?"

"Then that's all the more reason to get in and out of there as quickly as possible," Salcombe said.

I shook my head. I was trying to be optimistic, but the heavy weight of despair slowly sank onto my shoulders. I tried to reach out to Lessie as Salcombe turned his attention back to the books, but although I could feel the barest hint of her presence, she was too far away to communicate now. And even if she wasn't, what good would it do? She couldn't fly out of the valley, or contact Muza or any of the other dragons. Tavarian was all the way in Quoronis, and Carina, Rhia, and Jallis were in Zuar City. There was no way to call for help.

I wish I'd penned those responses before I left, I thought morosely as I sank into my chair. Because, try as I might to stay positive, I had a feeling those letters would have been the last my friends would have ever heard from me.

6

We arrived in Jedburgh with the setting sun, and despite my misgivings, I was glad to be on the ground again. Jedburgh was a charming, provincial town with half-timbered buildings, roads paved with perfectly cut square blocks of stone, and charming bridges that arced over the small river. It was smaller and quainter than Zuar City, but that also meant fresher air and cleaner streets, which I was grateful for.

"After taking your concerns into consideration," Salcombe said as the crew unloaded our luggage, "I have decided we shall pose as a Warosian couple, rather than Elantian. I suggest you speak as little as possible and let me do the talking, since your knowledge of both Warosian and Zallabarian are passable at best."

"You'd like that, wouldn't you?" I sneered as he reached into one of his pockets. I'd actually improved my Zallabarian quite a bit, but I saw no reason to tell Salcombe. But I quickly forgot all about that when he pulled out a jade-handled fan.

"Hey!" I protested as he snapped the fan open. He waved it once, and when he lowered it, he'd transformed himself. His graying hair was jet black now, his skin swarthy with a stubbled jaw, and his eyes a deep blue. "That's the fan Rajek tried to steal from me."

"Indeed, it is." Salcombe smiled, showing off his new dimples. He looked like a Warosian man in his early forties, and the sight of Salcombe wearing the face of a handsome man was surprisingly disconcerting. "I wanted it, so I had a middleman purchase it from your shop. I'm surprised you didn't decide to keep it for yourself—it's a useful item."

"Only if you make a habit of being two-faced," I sniped.

I half-expected Salcombe to insist I use the fan to disguise myself as well, but he didn't. I wondered if he worried that I would use it to make myself deliberately ugly—with the mood I was in right now, I was tempted to do it.

We finally disembarked from the airship and took a cab straight to the best hotel in town. Salcombe spoke to the front desk attendant in perfect Zallabarian, and we were immediately given a two-room suite that had been reserved in advance.

"You'll find more suitable clothing waiting for you," Salcombe said before he disappeared into his room. "Change into something more befitting your role and be back in the salon at six o'clock sharp. We will be dining with my contact in the private dining room downstairs."

"Fine." I entered my bedroom and slammed the door shut on the guard waiting outside. Salcombe was taking no chances—

he'd assigned two guards to follow me around at all times. They would sleep in the salon area of the suite, ready to escort me at a moment's notice.

Wanting some fresh air, I threw open the double doors on the far side of my bedroom and stepped onto the veranda. Flowering vines wrapped their way around the white balcony, lending a heady perfume to the evening air that soothed me, despite the frustration and despair eating at the corners of my mind.

Part of me was tempted to climb up onto the roof and run until my head was clear, until I was far, far away from Salcombe and his henchmen. But dinner was in less than an hour, and I had to be presentable. Besides, there was no point in running so long as Salcombe had the ability to track me. I needed to find a way to steal those locks of hair back from him. He undoubtedly had some stashed away in whatever hidey-hole he'd crawled into, but if I could take away the ones he had with him, I could evade him long enough to seek help and get to safety. Lessie's life was the only leverage he had, and if I wasn't within striking range of his men, he couldn't force me to do his bidding.

Back inside, I opened the closet to find several boxes of clothes waiting for me. There was an outfit similar to what I usually wore—a corset, leather pants, and boots—but the others held dresses and accessories. I grimaced at the soft pastels—unlike the gown Tavarian had once made me wear, these didn't even have pockets. How did Salcombe expect me to go hunting for treasure wearing these getups?

In the end, I decided to don the robin's egg blue one, which was a close enough match to the color of my eyes, and the least ridiculous. I pinned my curls to the top of my head with some gold hairpins I found in one of the smaller boxes, then slapped some color into my cheeks and headed out.

Salcombe waited for me in the salon, and he gave me a critical once-over. "You'll do," he said briskly, offering his arm. I took it reluctantly, and grimaced as I detected a hint of cologne on him. It was a sharp scent, and not one I was used to—Salcombe didn't wear perfume. But then again, he didn't wear sharp suits either, like the one he had on now. I guessed this was all just part of the façade he wanted to present to the man we were having dinner with.

When we got downstairs to the private dining room, a middle-aged man with silver-blond hair already waited. He wore a crisp three-piece black suit with a dark purple tie, and a thick walrus mustache that made him look stern and distinguished.

"Good evening, Mr. Trentiano," the man said in Zallabarian. "Is this your lovely wife?"

"It is," Salcombe said, giving the man a warm smile. Salcombe could turn on the charm when he wanted to, and the handsome façade he'd chosen for himself would only help. "Zara, this is Mr. Dieter Siegler, the property agent I spoke to you about. Mr. Siegler, my wife, Zara."

"Pleased to meet you," I said demurely.

"And you," Siegler said. "She is quite the beauty," he added to Salcombe. "You have done quite well for yourself."

"Indeed," Salcombe said with a laugh. "I am quite lucky." He squeezed my waist, a bit harder than necessary, intended as a warning.

I did my best to hide my annoyance as we were seated—I wasn't used to being talked about like a prized horse, especially not by Salcombe. While it was true that I was mostly a commodity for him, he had, for the most part, still treated me like a human being. As a child, one of the reasons I had liked him so much was because he'd treated me like an adult—someone with a working mind and skills that could be honed, rather than suppressed and scolded as the women at the orphanage had done. He had encouraged me to spread my wings and learn to fly.

Unfortunately, that encouragement had ended when I'd chosen to fly in a different direction than he'd wanted. And now he wanted to cage me, just like everyone else in my life had done. The reminder brought with it a sharp stab of betrayal, and I blinked back sudden tears.

How was it that things had gone so wrong between us? What would life have been like if Salcombe had been a bit more tolerant, and I a bit more flexible? Could we have had a real familial relationship? Would Salcombe still have gone to the dark side, seeking help from a god whose sole purpose was to bring death and destruction to our world?

Maybe, I thought, *but if things had gone differently, you might never have met Lessie.* And bringing Lessie into my life was something I could never regret, regardless of the circumstances.

Clearing my mind, I did my best to listen to Salcombe and Siegler's conversation. My Zallabarian wasn't perfect, so I couldn't quite understand everything they were saying, but I managed to get the gist as Siegler told us a bit about the properties Salcombe was interested in touring. I gathered from Siegler's tone of voice and the look in his eye that he was a bit suspicious of us as foreigners, but Salcombe affected the attitude of foolish but wealthy man who was willing to spend almost any sum on a property, "so long as my wife fancies it," he said, giving me a fond pat on my arm.

Oh, if only it were really up to me.

Convinced that there was an excellent chance that he would make a sizable profit, Siegler agreed to arrange a tour for us. Tomorrow, we would visit a country house with a garden and several large fields, and three townhouses in various nearby cities.

Two days, I thought as I ate. The food in my belly, which had been empty for close to forty-eight hours, was rapidly improving my mood, and I started to feel a bit more optimistic. Perhaps I could figure out a way to lengthen the time we spent here and give Lessie more time to catch up to us. I had no doubt she would risk the dangerous updrafts at the top of the cliffs to get to me, and I hoped she was strong enough to make it over the top safely. I wouldn't be able to forgive myself if anything happened to her on my account.

Sure enough, when I woke up the next morning, Lessie's presence was a bit stronger. Could it be that she made it over the cliffs? I tried to reach out to her, but she was still too far away to communicate with. I sincerely hoped I wasn't just imagining things.

I donned the same blue dress from the day before, and after a light breakfast, Salcombe and I set out in a carriage with Mr. Siegler. Two of the guards accompanied us as well, and while they wore more respectable clothing that hid their weapons, they still emanated an air of menace. Salcombe explained to Siegler that they were his bodyguards, and I briefly wondered how the man would react if I told him they were here to make sure I didn't escape.

He'd probably laugh it off as a joke, I thought morosely.

We started off with the townhouses first, the first two of which were a bust. There were plenty of valuables, but nothing even remotely approaching the value of a piece of heart. The third one, however, was far more interesting—as we passed through a parlor room on the second floor, I immediately sensed something valuable in the wall, and even though the distinct chime it gave off was nowhere near the powerful GONG I associated with the pieces of heart, I still itched to investigate it.

Salcombe immediately noticed the change in my mood. "Would you mind giving us a moment?" he asked Mr. Siegler. "I'd like to discuss something with my wife."

"Of course," Siegler said courteously. He withdrew to the lower floor, leaving us alone in the parlor room.

"Tell me what you've found," Salcombe said sharply.

"It's not the piece of heart," I said. "It's not valuable enough. But

I sense something behind here"—I pointed to a nearby book-shelf—"and I have a feeling there's something magical about it."

Briefly, I called up an image of the object in my mind. It was an ancient wooden box with steel locks, and though I couldn't actually see inside it, I sensed there were some spelled items within. I wondered if there was anything useful that I could use to escape Salcombe and his guards, if only I could get my hands on the items before they did.

Salcombe's face lit up, but before he could say more, a quavering voice cut him off. "Excuse me," the elderly lady who resided here said as she entered the room. "But will you be done touring the house? I have guests coming over soon."

"Mrs. Towins," Mr. Siegler said sternly as he bustled back in, "the property owner assured us that we would be free to tour the place from ten thirty until—"

"Don't worry about it," Salcombe cut in, giving the tenant a genial wave of his hand. "We're just finished anyway." Out of the corner of his mouth, he added to me, "We will come back later to retrieve this object. If it is magical, it could prove helpful in our quest." I could tell from the zealous glint that he hoped it actually *was* the heart, even though I'd told him otherwise.

We finished touring the townhouse, then visited the country house next. This was the place Salcombe had been certain the mage family had last resided, and he drew out this last tour as long as possible so I could scour every inch of the grounds, growing more and more frustrated when I turned up nothing.

"You'd better not be lying to me," he growled at one point when he'd taken me aside, his fingers digging into my upper arm. I'd had to hide my wince at his bruising grip—I kept forgetting how strong he was. How was he managing to keep up his strength like this if he didn't actually have the piece of heart with him? Was it some kind of spell? Or was possessing it enough to produce an effect on him?

By the time we finished, Salcombe was in a black mood.

Mr. Siegler said, "If you like, I'm sure I can find other properties for you to tour tomorrow—"

"No need," Salcombe said abruptly. "We have seen all we need to see. My wife and I will discuss, and let you know in a day or two which property we've decided on."

We returned to the hotel and immediately retired to the suite. "Rest for a bit," Salcombe ordered me, "and change into your normal clothes. We leave in an hour."

I didn't bother to ask where we were going—I already knew Salcombe wanted to head back to that townhouse. He ordered one of his guards to go out and fetch supplies, and he returned with hammers, pickaxes, and lanterns. Luckily, the townhouse was in the same city as our hotel, so it only took us thirty minutes to get there on foot.

"How are you planning to get around the old woman who lives here?" I whispered as we stood in the narrow alleyway on the south side of the building. "Are you just going to knock on her door and hope she's okay with you breaking down her wall?"

"Of course not," Salcombe said. He unhooked a small pouch

from his belt and handed it off to me. "You're going to go up to the roof and drop this down the chimney."

I snatched the pouch from Salcombe's spindly hand and opened it. Inside was a black powder, and one whiff of the heady scent made my head swim. "Sleeping powder?" I asked, yanking the drawstring shut.

Salcombe raised an eyebrow. "It's either that or kill her. Which would you prefer?"

"You're despicable." Shaking my head, I hooked the pouch onto my own belt, then made for the nearest window ledge and hoisted myself up. My skin crawled as I climbed up the side of the building, and I hesitated for the merest instant as I passed by the tenant's window. I could see the outline of her slight form as she slumbered in her bed, utterly oblivious to the fact that her home was about to be vandalized.

But it was better that she wake up to a giant hole in the wall than not wake up at all. So I gritted my teeth and climbed the rest of the way onto the roof. It wasn't hard to find the chimney flue, and after untying the pouch from my belt, I fished out a book of matches from my pocket.

Lessie could have lit this with a tiny snort, I thought as I lit the match and dropped it inside the pouch. The bag immediately began to smoke, and I quickly dropped it down the flue before I inhaled any of it and accidentally knocked myself out. My heart ached fiercely with longing at the thought of Lessie. I wished she were here now, so I could jump off this roof and onto her back, and the two of us could swoop down together and smite

Salcombe where he stood. Feeling for the bond, I thought she seemed a bit closer, but it was hard to tell.

"I did it," I muttered to Salcombe once I reached the ground. "Now what?"

"Now we wait."

We loitered outside for a good thirty minutes, waiting for the smoke to clear enough for us to enter the house safely. Even so, when we finally approached the door, one of Salcombe's goons handed out damp muslin cloths, and we tied them over our noses and mouths to block out any residual soot still in the air.

As we climbed up to the second floor, where I'd sensed the object the first time, my nerves began to ease, replaced by the familiar thrill I always felt when I was on the hunt for treasure. I could hear the object's call as clear as a bell in my head, and knowing it wasn't a piece of the dragon god's heart made me eager to find out just *what* it was, despite my misgivings about this whole thing.

"Zara." Salcombe's voice pulled me back to the present. He indicated the wall with his bony forefinger. "Where should he strike?"

I looked at the goon standing by the wall, holding a pickax in his meaty hands, and sent a silent apology up to the resident for what we were about to do. "Here," I said, indicating a spot in the middle of the wall. "The box is just below this spot, so be careful."

The man swung the pickax, and the wall crunched as it caved in.

Bits of dust and plaster clouded the air, and I was thankful for the cloth covering my face that shielded me from the worst of it. Waving our hands to dispel the debris, we waited until the cloud cleared before we approached.

"Looks like some kind of chest," Trolbos grunted. He took the pickax in his other hand and used it to widen the hole, then reached in and pulled out a wooden chest. It was the size of a small dog and secured with steel locks. Trolbos set it on a table, and Salcombe eagerly fished his lock picks out of his pocket.

"Let's see what's in here," he murmured, his eyes gleaming. But his delight quickly soured—the moment he tried to insert the lock pick into the keyhole, the hole disappeared. He pulled the pick back, and the hole reappeared, then disappeared again when he tried to insert it once more.

"Blast it," he growled after the third try. "There is some kind of spell on the chest. We'll need to take it back to the hotel so I can work on this properly."

We packed up and headed back to the inn, where Salcombe immediately set to work on breaking the box open. Sitting in one of the chairs by the fireplace, he set the box on the low table in front of him and called for one of his henchmen to bring a leather satchel that turned out to contain several magical items and ingredients. While Salcombe wasn't a mage, he often bought temporarily spelled items from mages that could be used in situations like these, to break open a resistant chest or vault, amongst other things.

Settling on the couch across from him, I decided not to tell

Salcombe I already knew what was in the box. Closing my eyes, I called up my mental image of the contents—a red leather-bound book, some jewelry, and a few trinkets. The magic on the box prevented me from seeing exactly what the trinkets were or what jewels were inside, but it didn't matter—my treasure sense told me that the book was by far the most valuable object inside.

"Aha!" Salcombe cried as the lock opened. It landed on the table with a heavy thud, and I sat up to peer into the box as he flipped the lid open. His eyes flickered with disappointment that there was no dragon heart inside, but open curiosity quickly replaced the look as he removed the leather book.

"This is written in ancient Zallabarian," he said, flipping through the pages. "A kind of diary."

"Hmm." I made a noncommittal sound in the back of my throat, trying to seem disinterested, and picked up the dagger instead. If Salcombe thought I was interested in the book, he would immediately start to scour every inch of it, and I was hoping he wouldn't look at it too closely. "This looks like one of those athames."

Salcombe looked up from the book and nodded. "Used in ritual ceremonies." He took the jeweled blade and studied it for a moment, then handed it back to me. "You could probably fetch a pretty price for it in your shop."

I raised an eyebrow. "You really think that after all this is over, I'm just going to go back to my shop and pick up where I left off?"

"Of course not," Salcombe said with a snort. "I was merely making conversation."

I rolled my eyes at him before examining the rest of the items—a small, magical mirror that showed only swirling colors on its silvered surface, a matching set of ruby and gold jewelry, and a purse full of old gold coins that would also fetch a nice price from the right collector. Salcombe gave these cursory glances, but to my dismay, he was far more interested in the book than anything else. He settled back into his chair and started to pore over it, hoping it would contain clues as to where to locate the other pieces of heart.

Sighing, I settled back on the couch again and stretched my legs across the cushions. A servant came in with glasses of warm, honeyed milk, and I took the one she offered me. Salcombe wasn't going to let me get my hands on that book until he was good and finished with it, so I took a deep drink and let the warm, sweet liquid flow down my throat. A drowsy feeling immediately swept over me, and I set it down on the side table, closing my eyes for a few minutes. Salcombe could wake me if he needed anything. After the day I'd had, I deserved a bit of shut-eye.

7

The sound of rotors spinning and wind rushing beyond the walls poked at my consciousness, pulling me out of a dead sleep. Groaning, I sat up and gritted my teeth. We were back on the airship again. A quick look out the window told me that we'd left Zallabar far behind, though the thick cloud coverage made it hard for me to see more than glimpses of the land below.

"You drugged me," I accused Salcombe, who was sitting on the bench seat across from me, still studying that blasted book.

"Of course I did," he said mildly. He turned the page, not bothering to spare me a glance. "You are far more manageable when you're unconscious, after all. I don't need to deal with your jabbering mouth or your tiresome objections."

I clenched my fists at my sides, wanting to tear into him. But there was no point in getting into a fight—clearly, I had no rights in Salcombe's eyes, and there was no use in trying to convince him otherwise. I would have to bide my time until I saw an opening to escape, and give him as few reasons as possible to lash out at me.

"So," I said after I'd counted to twenty and gotten my anger under control. "Have you found anything useful?"

"The book belongs to a mage called Mariyah Von Mahler," Salcombe said, finally raising his head to look at me. The excitement sparkling in his eyes made my stomach pitch. "From the dates in the book, it seems as though it is only four hundred years old, which makes me think she wrote in ancient Zallabarian only to make it harder for someone else to decipher the diary. There is priceless magical lore in here that many mages would give their right arm to have, but what is most interesting is the mentions of something important entrusted to the Mahler family. She seems quite confident that this mysterious object is well-protected, and that no one will ever be able to find it."

"You think it's the dragon heart?" I asked, infusing my tone with a hint of skepticism.

"There are several letters tucked in here that discuss the heart," Salcombe said. "One of them speaks of a family member that emigrated to Traggar, and possibly took the heart with him. There is even mention of a family name that is remarkably similar to the name of one of the original mages who broke the heart into pieces." His eyes sharpened. "Why? Do you have reason to think any of this information is incorrect?"

I lifted my left shoulder in a shrug, refusing to betray the knot of nerves in my chest. "I guess there's no way to know until you look into it some more, but it's not going to be easy. After all, Mahler's right, isn't she? We didn't find the piece of heart even though we were likely on her property."

Salcombe's eyes darkened. "Indeed," he said softly, and gestured to his men. They immediately yanked me out of my seat, holding my arms out to the sides.

"What are you doing?" I screamed, thrashing against them, but it was no use. They were extraordinarily strong, and they barely seemed to notice my glancing blows. Terror roiled in my gut as Salcombe rose from his chair, a needle in his hand.

"We are going to find out if you've been telling the truth."

He pricked the crook of my elbow with the needle, and I hissed. At first, I felt nothing but that tiny bit of pain, but a rush of giddiness quickly followed that, and I giggled as the drug hit my system. My head was crystal clear and my body felt relaxed, like I could sink back into the arms of the men who held me and let them carry me wherever they wanted. I trusted them. They were my friends. I could tell them anything.

"Set her back down," Salcombe said, and the men returned me to my seat. I stretched my arms across the back and grinned at Salcombe, happy to see him. But my heart plummeted into my stomach at the scowl on his face.

"What's wrong?" I asked, my insides twisting with anxiety. "Have I done something to upset you?" Salcombe was my oldest friend —I didn't want to make him mad. I wanted him to like me!

The angry look melted from Salcombe's face, and a wave of relief swept through me. "I'm not angry," he said, his face settling into a mask of indifference. It wasn't a smile, but that was okay—he usually looked like that anyway. "And I won't get angry with you, as long as you answer my questions truthfully."

"Of course!" An alarm bell went off in my head, but I immediately pushed it away. There was nothing to be afraid of. I was amongst friends. "I'll tell you whatever you want to know."

"Very good." Salcombe smiled, and I wanted to cheer. "Think back to yesterday, when we visited that old woman's townhouse. Did you sense any valuables on the premises?"

"Oh yes," I gushed, more than happy to answer. "She had lots of great stuff. There were some valuable paintings on the walls, and—"

Salcombe waved his hand, interrupting me. "The piece of heart, Zara. Did you sense it on the premises?"

"Oh no." My eyes widened. "I would have started with that. The pieces of the dragon god's heart sound very loud in my head—there's no way I would have missed it. I can usually sense anything if it's within a mile radius."

"Interesting." Salcombe raised his eyebrows, looking both surprised and impressed. "Have you always been able to do that?"

I shook my head. "Bonding with Lessie enhanced my treasure-sensing ability," I told him, "and Lord Tavarian helped me learn how to use it better." A pang of longing hit me as I remembered my dragon and my new mentor, and my skin crawled with an uncomfortable sensation. "I miss Lessie," I said with a sniff.

"You'll be reunited with her very soon," Salcombe said in a soothing voice.

I opened my mouth to ask how when something slammed into the side of the airship. My head rang as Salcombe and I smashed into the opposite wall, and panic sliced through me at the sight of a cut blooming on Salcombe's cheek.

"Are you all right?" I cried, lurching to my feet.

"Zara!" Lessie's voice cut through the mess of swirling emotions in my head, and I froze. *"Get to one of the starboard windows!"*

Before I could even think to respond, something smashed into the right side of the ship. I flew into the left wall, and my mouth dropped open as a large shape moved away from the side of the ship that had been hit. It was Kadryn. And on top of him...

"Jallis?" I cried.

"Get her!" Salcombe shrieked, his face purpling with rage. He pointed a shaking finger at me, his eyes wild, and terror gripped my throat as two of his men lunged at me. The serum Salcombe had pumped into me was wearing off fast, and I was starting to realize just how much trouble I was in. The ship was beginning to sink, dipping and leveling out at irregular intervals, making it hard to stand. Had one of the dragons punctured the air balloon?

I raised my hands to defend myself, but Jallis and Kadryn slammed into the ship again, knocking us all off our feet. As I struggled to get up, Lessie slammed her claws through one of the windows, spraying shards of glass everywhere.

"COME ON!"

Heart pounding, I scrambled to my feet and launched myself through the window. The bits of jagged glass cut my hands, but I barely noticed as I leaped into the air and onto Lessie's waiting back. Roaring, she thrashed her tail, slamming it into the side of the ship again just as Jallis and Kadryn dove. The airship spun to the side, plumes of black smoke marring the clear sky, and I held on tight as Lessie propelled us in the opposite direction with a mighty flap of her wings.

"Are you all right?" Jallis yelled, his dragon coming close so he could be heard over the wind. "You look a little out of it!"

"Did Salcombe hurt you?" Rhia, who I hadn't seen before, demanded. She flanked my other side as we watched the airship go down, descending in fits and starts. The pilot seemed to have enough control over the ship that he'd be able to land it with minimal damage, and I wasn't sure how to feel about it. It would be so much easier if Salcombe died in a crash, and yet...

"Zara?" Jallis said, sounding concerned. "Are you okay? Are you coherent enough to fly?" He reached out a hand, ready to pull me onto Kadryn's back so I could fly with him, as I'd done so many times in the past.

I shook my head, trying to clear some of the fog from my brain. "I'm fine," I shouted back. "Salcombe was interrogating me with a truth serum, but it seems to have mostly worn off." My head was starting to pound, the giddiness and sense of relaxation long gone. "What are you guys doing here?" Weren't they supposed to be at the academy? Dragon's Table was a long way from...well, wherever we were.

"We are still in Zallabarian territory," Lessie told me. *"Which is quite unfortunate, since this country seems to hate dragons. We'll need to get out of here as soon as possible."*

"Lessie told Kadryn you were in danger," Jallis told me, "and the two of us came as quickly as we could. But let's talk once we're back on the ground."

The three of us fell silent, and Kadryn and Ykos moved away, giving themselves and Lessie room to maneuver properly. *"Kadryn says that Jallis wants us to head for that hilltop,"* Lessie said, using her muzzle to indicate a tall, grass-covered mound less than a mile away.

"Let's do it," I agreed.

The three of us headed for the hill, and I leaned against Lessie, enjoying the smooth feel of her hide against my cheek. *"I'm so glad you came for me,"* I said. *"I'm guessing you managed to make it past the tops of the cliffs?"*

"I did." I felt a surge of pride in the bond. *"First try, too. I told you Tavarian was worrying for nothing."*

A giant grin spread across my face, and for the first time since I left Tavarian's secret estate, the gnawing anxiety that had plagued me finally removed its teeth from me. *"I missed you,"* I told her.

"Missed you, too."

We landed on top of the hill, which was wide enough to accommodate all three dragons, and yet small enough that we were still shielded by the hills and mountains that rose up all around us. Judging by the landscape, I guessed we were not far from the Elantian border.

Now that we were on the ground and didn't have to shout at each other, I told Jallis, Rhia, and Lessie about how Salcombe had kidnapped me, and what he wanted. "Luckily, we didn't actually find any pieces of heart," I told them, "but he still has those locks of my hair and can use them to track me down whenever he wants. He'll be coming for me again."

Lessie hissed at that, and Ykos and Kadryn let out low growls, echoing Lessie's sentiments perfectly. "I'd say that we ought to go after him and kill him once and for all, but I'm not sure that's wise," Jallis said, the corners of his mouth tightening with concern as he looked toward where Salcombe's airship had fallen. "We snuck out of the academy to get to you, which is bad enough as it is. If we end up causing an international incident when we're already on the brink of war, we'll be severely punished."

"And if Salcombe ends up resurrecting the dragon god, we'll all be dead," Rhia pointed out. "We can't just stand around and do nothing."

I bit my lip, conflicted. On the one hand, I didn't want to risk Rhia's and Jallis's lives, especially when they'd already put their lives and careers on the line just by coming out to rescue me. But on the other hand, Salcombe still had that book...

"You guys should return to the academy," I told Jallis and Rhia. "Now that I've got Lessie back, I should be fine on my own. Salcombe and I recently uncovered a book that has clues to the location of one of the pieces of heart. I have to get it back if I can, but there's no need for you to put yourselves in danger. You've already done the most important part—setting me free."

"Don't be silly." Rhia snorted. "What kind of friends would we be if we let you run off into danger by yourself? Of course we're coming with you."

"Rhia's right," Jallis said. "If you're going to do this, you shouldn't do it alone, and if you think getting that book back will stop Salcombe from finding another piece of the dragon god's heart, we should definitely do it. But if we're going to go after Salcombe, we should do it now, while the crew is still hurt and demoralized."

I nodded. "Salcombe is way too resourceful and clever to sit around long. We'll go after him now, but we'll have to be careful and make sure he doesn't see us coming."

"We should probably leave the dragons behind, then," Rhia said ruefully. Ykos let out a rumble of protest, but she patted his neck. "Sorry, buddy, but your stealth skills are useless on the ground."

"Not to mention that if any Zallabarians see our dragons, we're toast," Jallis said darkly. "Regardless of what happens, we need to be out of here in the next couple of hours. If the Zallabarians see dragons on their side of the border, they'll take that as a declaration of war, and then all bets will be off. In fact, we can't be sure they didn't already see us when we took that airship out."

I shuddered at the idea of being the ones responsible for setting off Zallabar while Tavarian was still trying to negotiate with Quoronis. I would never forgive myself if I put him in any danger, and the council wouldn't either. In fact, they'd probably roast us all.

Jallis and Rhia stripped off their dragon rider armor, and together, the three of us headed down the hill and into the nearby valley. We'd flown over a town nestled in the valley and hoped we might figure out where Salcombe and his crew had gone. No doubt, he would have headed for the nearest town to restock on supplies and nurse any wounds they had.

We decided to stop at the pub first, which in my experience was usually the best place to get information in any town. It was midafternoon, but the place was busy, the air humming with lively conversation as the inhabitants talked to each other in crisp, throaty Zallabarian. As we took our seats at one of the few empty tables and a server came to us, I felt a surge of gratitude for the language lessons I'd taken at the academy.

"A man with a group of mercenaries?" the server asked after Jallis had given her a description of who we were looking for. "I'm not sure, but I'll ask around."

She left to fetch tankards of ale and meat pies for us, and the three of us exchanged furtive glances. "I'm glad you two are doing the talking," I muttered. "You two are practically fluent. If I didn't know you, I'd assume you were natives."

Rhia smiled. "I'm sure you'll be up to speed in no time."

The server brought us our food, and we ate and listened to the conversations swirling around us, hoping to overhear something useful or that the server would bring back information about Salcombe. As expected, the most prominent topic of discussion was the impending war between Zallabar and Elantia, and the natives seemed very confident about their chances.

"Damn Elantians," a soldier grumbled, his thick mustache twitching with irritation. "They're getting far too bold. Did you see those dragons hovering at the border?"

"They don't take us seriously at all," another soldier said with a smirk. "But that's all about to change. When we blow a few holes in those dragon wings with our new cannons, they'll think twice about testing our borders again."

Jallis and I winced at the same time. We had been seen already. Anxiety clawed at me, and I reached out to Lessie in the bond. *"Is everything okay?"*

"We are fine. Bored, but fine."

"Stay on the ground," I ordered her. *"Someone has already seen the three of you. Don't let anyone find you."*

"We've already moved to the bottom of the hill, out of sight," Lessie assured me. *"We will be on alert for any humans in the area."*

"Sir?" The sound of the server's voice broke my concentration. "I believe I've found who you're looking for. Two of the city guards were just telling me they arrested a man traveling with four large, scary-looking men. He said the man goes by Trentiano, and he claims to be a businessman from Warosia. They are being held at the garrison, pending an investigation."

"Thank you," Jallis said. "That's very helpful."

"You are welcome." The server cocked her head. "May I ask why you are interested?"

"That man stole a priceless family heirloom from me," Rhia said, drawing herself up imperiously. "I have hired these two to help me track this man down and recover it." She turned to Jallis. "We should head down to the garrison immediately and speak to the guards before they set him loose."

The server raised her eyebrows. "Good luck with that," she said. "They are displaying the new cannons just outside, and there is quite a crowd."

Well, that settled it. We definitely had to go. Paying for our meal with one of the Zallabarian coins in Jallis's purse—apparently, he always carried a bit of currency from our neighboring countries in his purse just in case he found himself on a last-minute trip—we headed out of the pub and toward the garrison. There was no need to ask for directions—we simply followed the sound of the buzzing crowd, and quickly found ourselves in the center of town.

As the server had said, the new cannons were on full display—three of them, lined up neatly in a row, with a small group of soldiers guarding them. The local guards kept the crowd back at a safe distance to admire them, and it took a bit of time for the three of us to worm our way to the front to get a good look.

"They're small," Jallis said under his breath, careful to speak Zallabarian as we studied the artillery weapons in this crowd. "Three feet long, maybe?"

"Still too heavy to carry without cannon carriages," Rhia said, "but these are less than half the size of the cannons used in the last war. Do you really think they have enough firepower to shoot dragons out of the sky?"

One of the guards standing nearby must have overheard her, because he snorted and folded his arms. "These cannons might be smaller, but they're even deadlier than the ones we used in the last war against Elantia. Because they're so light and portable, it is much easier to maneuver them in any direction— important when fighting dragons when they're slithering through the air like winged serpents." His lips twisted in disgust, and I pressed my lips together as I felt a spark of indignation on my own dragon's behalf. "They also fire shrapnel munitions, which explode on impact."

I felt a distinct sense of derision from Lessie, who had been listening in. She scoffed at the idea of being taken down by shrapnel...but beneath her disbelief, I felt a heavy sense of unease. She was worried, and so was I.

"Ahhh." Jallis pretended to sound impressed. "That way they can inflict multiple wounds on the dragons."

"Exactly." The guard grinned fiercely. "Perhaps some of the older dragons with their tougher hides can withstand them, but it will be all too easy to shoot the newer ones out of the sky. Elantia has no idea what's coming."

Rhia and Jallis thanked the guard for the information, and we lingered for a few more minutes before carefully sliding back out of the crowd. "We should get back to our dragons now and get out of here," Jallis muttered.

I nodded in agreement. With all these guards and soldiers hanging around outside the garrison, there was no way we were getting to Salcombe. Hearts heavy, we trudged back up the valley to where our dragons were hidden. Dragon's balls, this was worse than we'd thought. Just how many cannons did the Zallabarian army have? They'd shown off three cannons here, and this was just a tiny town, barely worthy of a spot on the map.

"Zara!" Jallis hissed, grabbing my arm. "Over here!"

He yanked me behind a rocky outcropping on the trail just as a patrol of mountain soldiers came thundering by. They wore dark green uniforms with shiny gold buttons and were armed to the teeth with spears and swords. I shuddered as we watched them pass, close enough to smell the sweat and horsehair from their mounts. If they had taken a different turn, and come across our dragons...

We waited until we could no longer hear the hoofbeats, then raced into the woods to where our dragons waited by the hill. *"Time to go,"* I said as I vaulted onto Lessie's back.

"I know," she said. *"I saw the cannons through your eyes."*

Her words gave me pause, and I wondered if I was able to do the same thing—use our bond to see things through Lessie's point of view. But there was no time to ask. "Let's get out of here," I told the others.

We braced ourselves, and our dragons shot into the sky at the same time, beating their wings hard to gain velocity and altitude. Gripping the reins, I leaned forward on Lessie to move with her rather than battle the wind screaming in my ears to stay upright, and out of the corner of my eyes, I saw Jallis and Rhia do the same.

The sound of a loud explosion had me sitting up again, and I twisted around in my saddle to look back at the town. The soldiers had mobilized the cannons and were shooting at us!

"Evasive maneuvers!" Jallis shouted. The three of us immediately shot off in three separate directions, heading for the border as fast as we could. Clinging to the saddle for dear life, I held my breath as Lessie rolled to the side, evading more cannon fire. The screech of the wind stifled some of the explosion, but it still hurt my ears, and I wished I could clap my hands over them.

Note to self—get earplugs.

Ykos's roar distracted me, and I lifted my head to see blood streaming from a wound in his side. Rhia's face paled, and my stomach dropped into my boots as the dragon faltered in the sky. Immediately, Lessie swerved close, dropping ten feet below in case we needed to snatch Rhia out of the air.

But Ykos managed to level out, and though he slowed down, his wingbeats were still steady. Thankfully we seemed to be out of range of the cannons now, and Jallis and I kept close to the wounded dragon in case he needed assistance.

We didn't stop until we were well beyond the border, back in Elantian territory. Exhausted, we touched down in a clearing a few miles away from Zallabar, Ykos landing with a heavy thud.

"Oh no," Rhia moaned as she scrambled down her mount to study the wound. It was a large gash on Ykos's left side, and he groaned as he rolled onto his uninjured side, allowing his rider to take a better look.

"It's not very deep," Jallis said, giving Rhia a reassuring pat on the shoulder. "He should be able to heal that in a day or two, especially if I put a poultice on it."

He rummaged through his pack, but Lessie got to her feet and gently nudged both riders away with her snout. I could feel how exhausted she was as she approached, but she lay down on her belly next to Ykos anyway and gently licked the wound. The larger dragon made a rumbling sound that was half-pain, half-pleasure, and his entire body shuddered.

"I'd forgotten about the healing properties of dragon saliva," Jallis said quietly. The three of us watched in amazement as Lessie used her saliva to close the wound and stop the bleeding. "Unfortunately, it doesn't work on humans."

Lessie lifted her head and met my gaze with her fiery orbs. *I'm only able to close the skin,* she said, sounding apologetic. *"He will still need another day to knit the torn flesh back together."*

I told Jallis what Lessie had said, and he nodded. "We'll camp here tonight, then," he decided. "We're a bit closer to the border than I'd like, but there's no sense in injuring Ykos further by making him travel with that wound. We can all head back to the academy tomorrow."

Jallis strode off into the woods, unslinging his crossbow from his back so he could catch dinner for us. While we waited for him to return, Rhia and I built a fire, using a thin stream of flame from Lessie to light the pile of logs and kindling we'd found. We also set out the bedrolls they had brought—one for each of them, and Rhia had even brought an extra one for me.

"I don't know how to thank you," I told her as we sat down on the small logs we'd dragged into the clearing to serve as benches. "You and Jallis saved my butt."

"Of course we did." Rhia smiled. "That's what friends do. I have no doubt that if our positions had been reversed, you would have done the same, even if that meant having to blast through half the council to do it."

I gave her a crooked smile. "True. I've never been much for the rules. I guess I'm just not used to people looking out for me much. I've always been the one who looked out for everyone else, because I was more fortunate." My orphan friends helped me out when they could, but they'd had their own burdens to struggle with, and I wasn't into the habit of dumping my problems on other people anyway. "The only person in my life aside from Carina who I could come to for help was Salcombe, and asking for help from him was always a double-edged sword."

Rhia's smile melted into a sympathetic expression, and she scooted closer so she could hug me. "I'm sorry things have turned out this way, Zara," she said. "I know it can't be easy, making an enemy of the man who acted as your father figure for so long."

I snorted. "I didn't make an enemy out of him. *He* made an enemy out of *me* the moment he tried to have me killed." I shook my head. "I'm an idiot for caring about him at all. He's proven to me on more than one occasion that I'm just something for him to use and discard."

"Just because Salcombe is a cold, unfeeling asshole doesn't mean you have to be," Jallis said as he strode back into the clearing. A large, turkey-like bird was slung across his shoulder—enough to feed all three of us, and then some. "You have a big heart, Zara, and that's a strength, not a weakness."

I smiled as Jallis's words warmed my chest. "You two always seem to know just the right things to say," I said as I got to my feet.

Jallis's eyes twinkled. "That's why we're your friends."

I knew from the tone in his voice and the way he looked at me that he wanted to be more than friends, and my lips tingled as I remembered the last time he'd kissed me. Only a few weeks ago, I realized with some surprise. I'd thought that it would be a lot longer until I saw him again, and part of me wanted to gravitate toward him, to wrap my arms around his neck and see if his lips were as soft as I remembered, if his touch would still fill me with that easy warmth that was so inviting. But Rhia was here, and somehow I doubted she'd be amused if Jallis and I engaged in a make-out session when there was cooking to be done.

The three of us got to work, plucking and dressing the bird, then sticking it on a makeshift spit to roast over the fire. It took a few hours to cook the bird, so while we took turns turning it over the flame, we talked about what we'd seen.

"I can't believe they managed to hit Ykos from so far away," Rhia said as she sat down next to Ykos. She stroked her hand over his scales, careful to keep away from his injury, and he let out a contented rumble not unlike a purring cat. "That soldier was right about the shrapnel bombs. They only had three cannons out there today, but what if we came up against more? If two or three of those had hit Ykos at the same time, or if even one of them had gotten his wings, we would have gone down."

"I know." Jallis's voice was low, his normally cheerful face somber. He ran a hand along the outside of Kadryn's left wing, and the large dragon twitched. "I think they designed those cannons with that in mind. Wings are the most fragile part on their body—the membranes are thinner, and the tendons have less protection."

"Then we'll just have to be faster than the cannons," Lessie huffed, tossing her head. *"There is no point in sitting here, cowering in fear over what might happen. If these Zallabarians decide to take our country, we have to fight."*

Ykos rumbled in agreement, but Kadryn snorted, annoyed. "That's all well and good," I said aloud, "but I think it's stupid of us to continue to use dragons to fight when the enemy has airships and long-range cannons now. We should be investing our gold into increasing our technology and weapons capabilities, as the other countries have been doing."

"I agree," Rhia said grimly. "With our dragon population dwindling, it is only a matter of time before the other countries are able to overwhelm us completely."

Jallis looked torn. "I think dragons and their riders still bring a lot to the table during wartime," he said, "but I don't deny that relying on dragons alone is an outdated, and also harmful strategy. If Quoronis and Traggar do ally with Zallabar, and Zallabar gives them these new cannons, there's no way we'll survive. Cannons are a lot easier to make than dragons."

"Not to mention that dragons are too precious to be used as disposable cannon fodder," I pointed out. "Zallabar's population is nearly double ours—they have no lack of soldiers to send into battle. But we can't just send our dragons out to be blasted to bits in the sky. I won't have it." I wrapped my arm around Lessie's neck and hugged her, my heart clenching. The idea of her being hurt or killed by some enemy cannon fire, over some stupid war...

"I wouldn't say that our dragons are cannon fodder," Rhia protested. "These days they are mostly just used for special occasions."

"That's because we haven't gone to war in a long time," I argued. "And now that we're on the brink of it, we're falling back into our old ways. Elantia needs to stop clinging to old traditions and move into the future." I shook my head, bitterness seeping into my voice. "I never imagined I'd be sitting out in the middle of nowhere, talking about war and the fate of our country with two sky-dwellers. All I ever wanted was to be a treasure hunter."

Jallis's eyes flashed. "It's impossible to escape the impact of war," he said, a bit stiffly. "Even if you'd never become a dragon rider, you'd be affected. A war between Zallabar would affect trade and the ability of citizens to travel between countries. It would certainly have put a crimp on your treasure hunting."

I winced at Jallis's sharp words and the hurt look on Rhia's face. "I'm sorry," I said. "I didn't mean for it to come out that way. I know war affects everyone, and I want to do whatever I can to stop it from happening and protect our people. It's just...frustrating. And I'm tired, and just coming off a kidnapping from the man who used to be my father figure."

Jallis's eyes softened and he stepped toward me. "It's been a tough day for all of us, but especially for you."

I allowed him to sweep me into a hug and sank into his embrace. Jallis was warm and comforting, his scent clean even beneath the sweat clinging to his skin. A large part of me wanted to burrow into him and never let go, but I allowed him to draw me back down to the logs so we could sit and finally eat some of the meat we'd been cooking. Lessie's stomach grumbled loudly as Jallis began to cut pieces off the carcass, and she and Kadryn got to their feet.

"We're going hunting," Lessie informed me. *"We'll bring back something for Ykos, too."*

"Okay." I didn't move from the log, but I reached out and gave her a mental stroke through the bond. *"Stay safe."*

While the dragons hunted and we ate, Jallis and Rhia quizzed me about my time with Tavarian. Where had he taken me?

What kind of training had we done? What was it like living alone with him for weeks on end? I laughed as I answered their incessant questions, telling them what I could, deflecting what I couldn't. Now that we weren't talking about war anymore, we fell back into that easy sense of camaraderie. This sensation of closeness, of belonging, was something I hadn't felt much of before I became a rider, and now that I was back with my friends again, I realized I'd missed it.

"Lord Tavarian is going to lose his mind when he comes back from Quoronis and learns about everything that's happened while he's been gone," Jallis said, shaking his head. "He never should have left you and Lessie alone."

"He couldn't have taken us with him, and there was no time for him to escort me back to the academy," I said, feeling a bit defensive of Tavarian. The man had done so much for me; it didn't feel right to let Jallis talk badly about him. "I'm sure that if he'd known Salcombe was able to track me, he would have made different arrangements, but as far as we knew, staying at the hidden location was the safest thing to do."

"Fair enough," Rhia said. "But now that we know Salcombe can track you, what can we do? We can't wait for Tavarian to resurface."

"You'll have to come back to Dragon's Table," Jallis said. "Being close to the other dragon riders, who will be able to protect you, is the safest option."

I sighed. "I know that, but I don't think Headmaster Caparro will be thrilled about having me, since I'm a hunted woman. And I hate the idea of sitting around and waiting for Salcombe to find me. I want to take the fight to him."

We argued about it for a bit longer, then retired to our bedrolls. Curling up against Lessie's side, I closed my eyes and tried to relax, but my mind still raced. Going back to Zuar City and Dragon's Table was all well and good, but Salcombe would only come after me, and that's where all my friends lived. How could I safeguard my business and my friends, and still protect Lessie? Salcombe wouldn't hesitate to use any of them against me, and I especially didn't want to involve any of the orphans, who had so little. Sure, Salcombe was being detained by Zallabarian authorities, but he'd worm his way out of that situation in a day or two. He would manage to convince them that he was Warosian, not Elantian, and they would let him go.

What if he decides to ally with the Zallabarians against Elantia? a worried voice in my mind asked. Salcombe had a lot of knowledge and experience—he could do quite a bit of damage, and if he thought allying with Zallabar was the quickest way to get the remaining pieces of the dragon heart, he would do it without hesitation.

But deep inside, I knew that would be a last resort for Salcombe. He was a loner at heart, used to being in charge and doing things his own way. He wouldn't want to have to work with someone else to get what he wanted, especially not a head of state from another country.

Would Salcombe be able to enjoy the newfound health his piece of heart provided him with indefinitely? Or would the strength eventually fade if he didn't find more pieces? If I were the dragon god, I would have set it up that way, so Salcombe would be forced to collect the rest of them. What would happen if I stole the piece of heart he already had? He didn't keep it on him, which must mean he had it tucked away in one of his many hiding places. If I got my hands on the heart, would I be able to sever whatever bond it had with Salcombe and weaken him again?

"I like that idea," Lessie said, butting into my thoughts. *"We should do it. If Salcombe no longer is in possession of the heart, that will likely sever his connection with the dragon god. Perhaps he might even come back to his senses without Zakyiar's influence."*

"I'd love to do that," I told her, *"but I have no idea where to start."*

"You know Salcombe better than anyone else," Lessie reminded me. *"Perhaps there is some hidden clue in your mind you just aren't yet aware of."*

I pondered that idea as I stared at the stars, wondering if I subconsciously already had the answer to the piece of heart's location. But even though I wracked my brain, going over all my conversations with Salcombe through the years, I couldn't find anything. I eventually slipped into a restless, unsatisfying sleep where I wandered a series of dark corridors and wondered if I would ever find the light that would lead me out of this never-ending maze.

8

The next morning, we sat around the fire and ate the remnants of last night's meal while discussing our next move. Ykos was doing much better already, and we were confident he'd be able to fly without pain in a few hours. In the meantime, he was resting comfortably while Kadryn and Lessie flew around the area, checking for threats and likely hunting as well. Dragons grew throughout their entire lives, and as a young dragon who was only a few months old, Lessie's appetite was especially voracious.

"So," I asked Rhia and Jallis, "I was thinking last night while I was trying to sleep, and I've decided the best thing I can do while I wait for Tavarian to come back is to return to Zuar City and see if I can track down Salcombe's piece of heart."

"Do you really think it's in the city?" Jallis asked, sounding surprised. He scratched his chin, which was lightly stubbled and gave his normally clean-cut appearance a bit of a roguish look that I quite liked. "I would have thought Salcombe would hide it as far away as possible, or even in another country entirely."

"It's very likely," I said, "but Salcombe loves Zuar City, and even though he had to abandon his primary residence, I'm sure he has another hidden one somewhere." Zuar City was huge—over one hundred and fifty square miles—and there were plenty of places he could have hidden his stuff. "I have to return to the city anyway, so I might as well make myself useful, and even if he isn't storing the heart in Zuar City, I may still find some clues that could help us thwart his efforts."

"That's all well and good, but I don't think the academy will let you go hunting for it at night," Jallis pointed out. "They're going to want you to stay on the school grounds. In fact, they may not even let you visit your shop."

"Which is why I'm not going back to the academy," I said. "I'll need to find a place to lay low that has room for Lessie. I was thinking maybe Tavarian's place—"

"You and Lessie can stay with me," Rhia offered promptly. Jallis looked like he wanted to protest, but she kept right on talking. "My family home isn't as big and grand as Tavarian's, but it is secure, and my mother will be more than happy to have you. You shouldn't stay somewhere alone, Zara, not when we know Salcombe will try to come for you again."

"But isn't your family home on Dragon's Table?" I asked, biting my lip. "I guess we'll just have to come in at night so the guards don't recognize Lessie and me."

Jallis sighed. "I do think that you would be better off just staying at the academy and waiting for Tavarian to come back," he said. "But if this is what you want to do, of course I'll support you. We'll just tell the headmaster that we returned you to Tavarian's hidden estate."

My stomach twisted with guilt at the heavy note in his voice—I knew that Jallis wasn't the type to lie to his superiors, and this couldn't be easy for him. "Thank you," I said, wrapping my arms around his neck in a hug. "This means a lot to me."

Jallis hugged me back. "I just want you to be safe," he said, his face pressed into my hair. "And I know that if you can find Salcombe's piece of heart and get it away from him, it'll make it that much harder for him to come after you again."

He stroked a hand down my back, and I felt that familiar stirring of warmth low in my belly. It would be so easy to tilt my head back and let him kiss me. But Rhia was sitting right there...

Jallis seemed to sense my thoughts. He pulled away and gave me a rueful smile. *Maybe next time,* he seemed to say as he squeezed my hand.

The dragons returned with two trozla carcasses in their jaws and immediately sat down to feast in the clearing. The additional food seemed to give Ykos a burst of energy, and after they were finished, he decided to take to the air and do a few experimental circles in the sky.

"I think he's about ready to go," Rhia said after he'd landed again, smoothly and without a hint of discomfort. She scratched behind one of his horns, and he let out a loud rumble of contentment. "If we leave now, we should reach Zuar City by dark."

Decided, we took to the skies and headed for home. Now that we were back in our own borders, the six of us were far more carefree as we soared over fields and hills, passing by towns that would normally take us days to travel to. Man, I loved flying so much. Racing across the rooftops had been the closest I'd been able to get to it before I became a rider, and part of me wondered if I'd loved it so much because my dragon rider blood had wanted to be as high up as often as possible.

"I don't know how I survived without you," I told Lessie as I stroked the side of her neck.

She let out a rumble of contentment. *"It's a shame that you never knew your parents. I wonder why they were living in the lower city, when at least one of them had to be a dragon rider."*

Instinctively, I reached for the dragon blade Jallis had given me, before remembering with dismay that it was still at Tavarian's estate, along with my lock pick and other valuables. That blade was the only thing in existence that linked me to my past—it had been part of Jallis's family collection, and when I'd picked it up, it had responded to me instantly, keyed to my family's blood. Jallis had admitted to me that his father had picked it up recently, which meant that I wasn't part of the Lyton family, as I'd initially feared, but some other house entirely. I wondered if Lord Lyton, Jallis's father, would be willing to tell me where he'd gotten it. Tracing the ownership of the blade was the easiest way to determine which family it had originally belonged to.

Except you can't visit Jallis's father, because his mother hates your guts, I told myself. *You're trying to keep a low profile, remember?*

I'd have to put that on the to-do list for later. Luckily, it wouldn't take more than a few days to search the city and its surrounding environs—the pieces of heart all made a very distinctive, loud sound if I came within a mile of them. It was very likely Jallis was right, that Salcombe had hidden the heart somewhere else. If that was the case, I would have to go back to the academy and regroup. Perhaps once Tavarian returned, I could convince him to let me form some kind of search party, but until then it would be foolish for me to scour the entire country by myself. The last thing I needed was for Salcombe to smuggle one of those portable cannons across the border so he could shoot Lessie and me out of the sky.

"That will never happen," Lessie said fiercely. *"If he shows his bony face again, I'll blast him with my dragon fire before he can get off a single shot."*

"I have no doubt, but I'd rather not take the risk."

Since Lessie and Ykos were still not strong enough to fly such long distances, we stopped halfway through the trip to rest. Recognizing the patch of forest we flew over, with its orange-trunked trees, as the location of the hidden palace, I had us stop there so I could pick up a few artifacts for the shop.

"So, *this* is where you guys went the first time you flew together?" Rhia asked as we descended the rope ladder that hung from the edge of the giant hole in the forest floor. "To an underground palace from the Golden Age?"

"Yep," Jallis said as he helped me to the ground. "As far as first dates go, I have to say it's the most unusual one I've been on."

"I wish someone would take *me* on a date like this," Rhia said as she looked around the room. The cavernous space was precisely how I remembered it—with a coffered dome hanging above us, hidden from the world by a thick carpet of loam and grass, and floors and walls of pure marble covered in vines.

"Isn't that what we're doing right now?" I teased, looping my arm through Rhia's. I led her down the long hall and through an archway that led into another room that sported the faded remnants of frescoes on its walls.

"Yes, it's very romantic," Rhia said dryly. "Are we going to have a candlelit dinner after this?"

I only smirked, and Rhia quickly fell silent as we walked through rooms upon rooms filled with statues and furniture and all kinds of ancient paraphernalia. The art in here was remarkably well preserved, since the place had been sealed off from the outside world for so long, but now that an earthquake had caved in several sections of the ceiling, I knew it was only a matter of time before nature reclaimed this place. I'd come here as often as I could over the years to rescue the wealth of art and artifacts hidden inside, but as a one-woman show, it had been hard to take very much at a time, especially since I was trying to keep this place a secret. But now that I had Lessie, I might very well be able to get more done around here once she'd grown bigger.

We didn't spend too much time in the underground palace, just long enough for me to grab a few items, including a couple of beautifully carved animal statuettes and a set of gem-studded ritual goblets—items light enough for Lessie to carry without slowing her down, but would fetch a very high price. Since I would have to carry these through the city myself, I couldn't afford to take anything big—Lessie would create quite a spectacle if she brought me into Zuar City herself, and news of our return would undoubtedly get back to the guards at Dragon's Table.

We reached Zuar City just as the sun was setting, and the three of us perched on a hillside to wait for night to fall. "It's so beautiful," Rhia sighed as we watched the gas lamps being lit, one by one. As the sun disappeared from the horizon, painting the vermillion sky with shades of indigo and navy, the lamps began to twinkle like fallen stars.

"It really is," I said. Standing out here, so far removed from the inner workings of the city, it was hard to reconcile the image of the bright, sparkling city with the underbelly of poverty and scum that existed beneath the surface. I made a mental note to check on the orphans tomorrow, after I'd gotten an update from Carina. We'd employed several of the orphans, but many others were still on the streets. The orphanage only kept children until they were around sixteen, then unceremoniously kicked them out to fend for themselves. Many of them lacked specialized skills to get good jobs, so they often resorted to begging or prostitution.

"Well, I guess it's time to get going," Jallis said when night had finally fallen completely. "Are you going to start your search tonight?"

"No." Tonight I would catch up with Carina and the shop, and let Lessie rest after a long day of travel. Stepping closer to Jallis and Rhia, I pulled two items out of one of Lessie's saddlebags. "Thank you so much for helping Lessie and me. I don't know what I'd do without you two. Please take these as tokens of my gratitude."

"Oh no, we couldn't—" Rhia began, then stopped as I placed a lovely gold-plated lamp in her hands. She had admired it when we were in the palace, and I'd quietly taken it to give to her later. "Never mind. I'm definitely taking this home."

I laughed, hugging her, then turned to Jallis. "I thought this might come in handy." I handed him a small gold compass decorated with tiny sapphires.

Jallis's eyes lit up. "It's a wonderful gift," he said, studying the compass for a moment. He put it into his pocket, then wrapped his arms around me. "But there's something else I want more."

He kissed me, and my whole body seemed to sigh, relaxing into his warmth. Twining my arms around his neck, I leaned into the kiss, our mouths moving gently together as we familiarized ourselves with the shape of each other's lips. His tongue teased the seam of my mouth, and I opened just enough to let him in.

Rhia groaned. "Do I need to find you two a room?"

Jallis chuckled, withdrawing. "You could always make yourself scarce," he said, waggling his eyebrows.

Rhia snickered. "As if. Someone needs to be around to chaperone you two." She slid her foot into one of Ykos's stirrups and launched herself into the saddle. "Now let's get our red-haired princess back to her tower."

We flew over the city, high enough that our dragons blended into the inky sky. Stars blazed above us, and the night wind whipped my hair around my face, a siren's call. As we approached the Treasure Trove, Lessie dipped lower, and I felt a pang of regret. I wished I could stay up here with her. I loved my shop, but I wasn't ready to leave Lessie yet, not when I'd spent the past few days wondering if I would ever see her again.

"You're not leaving me," she said softly, rubbing up against me through the bond. *"So long as we're connected, we will never truly be apart."*

Nodding, I stroked her scales. *"Love you,"* I said, and then dropped off her back.

9

I landed on the Treasure Trove's rooftop soundlessly, thanks to my spelled boots, which Salcombe hadn't taken from me. I clutched the bag of artifacts to my chest and watched as Lessie and the other two dragons soared upward and curved around, heading for Dragon's Table. Rhia would get Lessie settled at her family manor, and then she and Jallis would return to the academy.

I just hoped they wouldn't be punished for taking an unauthorized leave of absence. Especially since they didn't have any *actual* proof that they'd saved me.

If they do get punished, I'll make sure to go up there and set things right, I decided as I climbed down from the roof. If anyone deserved to be penalized for this mess, it was me, not them.

On the ground, I turned to the storefront and was pleased to see Kira, Tiana, and Nate in the shop with Carina, helping her close up for the night. The two guards standing by the front door jerked in surprise, and immediately moved to block it.

"Sorry, miss," one of them said gruffly. "The shop is closed."

I folded my arms across my chest. "I own the shop. Now let me in."

The guards hesitated as they studied me, their eyes lingering on my hair. "They said she had red hair, didn't they?" one of them asked.

"She just dropped down from the roof," the other one said. "She's probably a thief, just trying to—"

"Zara!" Carina's shocked voice drew their attention away. She stood behind the storefront window, clutching a giant silver platter in her hands. I grinned at the stunned look on her face. "What are you doing here?"

"Trying to visit my own shop," I called through the glass. "You want to call your dogs off?"

The door burst open, and Carina pushed past the guards. "When did you get back?" she cried as she flung her arms around me. "I thought you were going to be away for months!"

"Zara!" the others called, their voices ringing with joy. Nate scrambled out the door to hug me as well, Kira and Tiana not far behind. "What are you doing here?"

"It's a bit of a long story," I said. "Why don't we go inside so I can tell you all about it?"

We went into the shop, and I immediately handed Carina my

finds from the underground palace. "I made a stop on the way back to bring these for you. They should all fetch a good price."

"Excellent." Carina immediately handed them off to Kira, who took them into the back to be cataloged and prepped for sale. "Dragon's fire, you look exhausted, Zara. Have you eaten anything today?"

I thought about it, and my stomach rumbled loudly. "Not since this morning," I said. "I could use a bite."

"Nate, Tiana, head out and see if you can scrounge up a late dinner for us." Carina flipped them a coin. "While they go get the food, you can wash up and change into something more comfortable." She eyed my dirty clothes.

I sniffed my armpit and wrinkled my nose. "I could definitely use a shower," I decided.

Carina followed me upstairs. "Don't freak out on me," she said as I opened the door, "but I've been letting Tiana and Nate use your apartment, and they've brought a couple of things over."

"No kidding," I said as I walked into the bedroom. It looked like someone had set off a pink explosion—my sheets had been stripped away and replaced with pink satin, and there were white and pink knickknacks everywhere in the room. "Not exactly what I was expecting to come home to."

Carina winced. "If we'd known you were coming back, I would have had Tiana fix the room up and brought her and Nate to my place until she found a permanent place to stay," she said. "The two of them have been saving up to move out—"

I held up a hand. "Please, don't apologize," I said. "I'm happy you've put the space to good use, and I'm not moving back in permanently anyway. I'm only here for a few days."

"Why—" Carina started, and then shook her head. "No, get yourself cleaned up and changed. I'll be in the living room."

I was more than happy to follow Carina's suggestion, stripping out of my clothes and heading into the shower. The hot water felt fantastic as it hit my face, and I stood under the spray for far longer than necessary as I allowed the water to soothe away the stress clinging to my body.

When I finished, I rummaged through the closet for something to wear. Most of my clothes were at Tavarian's secret estate, but I was able to scrounge up a pair of loose pants and a black shirt.

When I came back out to the living room, the scent of roasted meat and grilled vegetables hit me.

"The butcher was in his shop, and he took pity on us," Tiana said from the stove as she grilled meat and vegetables. Within no time, she was setting plates on the counter heaped with food. "Now, why don't you grab a plate and fill us in?".

I did exactly that, and we sat together on the couches and chairs while I told them what had transpired between eating bites of Tiana's delicious cooking. The three of them asked questions here and there, but mostly they stayed silent as I told them about Salcombe's kidnapping, and my decision to return home instead of going to Dragon's Table.

"So, you're here to try and find Salcombe's piece of heart?"

Carina asked when I'd finished. "You really think it's here in the city?"

I shrugged. "I don't know, but since I'm stuck here anyway, I might as well try to find it. Have you seen any sign of him?"

"No." Carina shook her head. "The guards haven't noticed anything suspicious. I don't think he's tried to approach the shop."

"I can ask our friends to keep an eye out," Tiana said. "Is there anything specific we should be looking for?"

"Black-robed men with a silver dragon on their chests," I said. "Those are Salcombe's...acolytes." I twisted my lips in a grimace at the very idea that Salcombe had zealous followers, like his own cult, but that's what it was. "Salcombe himself might be in disguise, as a dark-haired, handsome man in his forties. He used a magic fan to change his appearance while we were in Zallabar."

"A magic fan?" Carina's eyes narrowed. "You don't mean..."

"Yep. The same fan Rajek tried to steal from me." That fan had become the bane of my existence, and I had half a mind to burn it if I ever got my hands on it again.

Carina shook her head in disgust. "He can disguise himself to look like anyone, then," she complained. "How are we supposed to guard against that?"

"He can change his appearance, but not his build or his height," I told her. "And although he can be charming, his mannerisms are there if you know what to look for. Besides, I doubt you'll be seeing Salcombe himself anytime soon.

Tiana promised she and the other orphans would keep an eye out for any man or woman matching that description, and Carina would let me know if anyone came into the shop mentioning either Zakyiar or the heart. I informed her that I'd help out with the shop in the afternoons, and everyone was overjoyed to hear it.

After we'd finished eating and catching up, we all retired early to get a good night's sleep. Since Nate usually slept on the couch, I slept with Tiana in my bed, which was a bit strange, especially with the foreign sensation of satin sheets beneath me. But I was exhausted from my recent trials, and after checking in with Lessie that she was settled in and saying a sleepy good night to her, I quickly fell asleep.

The next day was a busy one. Despite Carina's initial complaints that the guards were driving business away, we had quite a few customers and treasure hunters in the shop, buying and selling goods. Not wanting to alert the citizens that I'd returned, I stayed in the back of the shop while Kira and Nate brought me new finds to authenticate and do valuations on. I found myself so busy with all the traffic that I barely had time to eat, and by the time night fell and the shop closed, I was downright grumpy.

"It would be nice if we could take on another authenticator," I said as Carina and I ate dinner in the back while the others closed up shop. "Have you been teaching the orphans anything?"

Carina sighed. "They're so busy with their other tasks that I haven't had time," she said. As the daughter of an explorer herself, Carina had enough experience to be able to tell whether or not an artifact or piece of art was genuine, though of course she didn't have my treasure sense. "I suppose I really should hire some more employees to help out, but I guess I'm still nervous that this is just a fluke and business will dry up. I'd hate to hire a bunch of people and give them hope only to fire them again."

"I get what you're saying, but it's obvious we need help, and there are so many orphans out there who need the money," I told her. "I'm not going to let this shop fail, Carina. Even if I have to give up life as a dragon rider and go back to treasure hunting."

Her eyes widened. "Can you even do that? Would they let you?"

I gave her a crooked smile. "Let's hope we never have to find out."

After we finished closing up for the day, I went back up to my room to nap for a few hours. I was having a pleasant dream when Lessie's consciousness nudged against mine, rousing me from my slumber.

"Come on, sleepy. It's time to go hunting."

Instantly, I was wide awake, my blood humming with excitement at the thought of riding my dragon. I pulled on my boots, double-checked that I had my gear, then climbed out of the window and up to the rooftop where Lessie waited.

"Hey." I wrapped my arms around her neck and pressed my face against her warm scales. *"How was it, staying at Rhia's place?"*

"Her mother is a gracious host," Lessie replied as she wound her neck around me, pressing her cheek against my back as she returned the hug. *"And the stable is spacious and clean. However, since they were not expecting another dragon to be in residence, they do not have quite enough food to feed me. I will need to go hunting after we are finished here tonight."*

I bit my lip. *"I'd rather not have you roaming the countryside without me,"* I said as I mounted her.

Lessie let out a disgusted rumble. *"I am not a pet to be coddled and sheltered. I am a dragon, and I smite my enemies with fire and fang."*

"I know." I patted her neck. *"But I'd feel a lot better if you stayed close. Let me see if I can figure out a solution, and if not, you're free to go and hunt."*

Lessie made a noise of agreement in the back of her throat, and with a powerful flex of her wings, we were in the sky. I lifted my face to the wind as we soared upward, gliding over the vast sea of rooftops and flickering lights. Normally, I would have urged Lessie higher, so she could hide amongst the clouds, but I needed her to stay relatively close to the city so that I could use my treasure sense.

Closing my eyes, I opened up my senses. Immediately, I was overwhelmed by a cacophony, and I gritted my teeth against an instant headache. Sucking in a breath, I filtered out the lower value items, trying to narrow it down so I could hear the higher priced objects more clearly. But there were so many different items here in the crowded city that it was difficult, and it took quite a while before the smaller items finally faded away.

"Nothing here," I said to Lessie.

Lessie and I spent the next couple of hours slowly flying over the city while I tried to use my senses to locate the heart. It was much more difficult than either of us had anticipated—the level of control needed to keep up a slow, steady pace was not something Lessie had much experience with, and as I moved into the more affluent parts of the city, it became harder to filter out items. I'd thought this would be easy, since the dragon heart was so much more powerful and valuable than anything else, but there were so many other items of varying values in the city that its signature, if it was even here, was easily muffled.

But even though the hunt was frustrating, Lessie and I enjoyed the ride. I'd always enjoyed looking down at the city from the rooftops, but getting a bird's eye view from the back of a dragon was another experience entirely. Yes, I could see the bad up here —muggers skulking in the shadows, waiting to pounce on unexpected victims, a prostitute servicing a john in an alley, two men getting into a fistfight outside a bar—but there were also the more charming aspects, like the couple cuddling on their terrace beneath the moonlight, the trio of cats caterwauling in concert on the back of a fence, the light and music spilling out of the open door of a pub.

Eventually, Lessie began to tire, and I looked for a safe place where she could set down without collapsing a roof or terrorizing sleepy, unsuspecting citizens. *"Land here,"* I told her, pointing to a secluded area of the city park. Lessie did as I asked, setting down on a wide patch of lawn fifty yards away from a children's playing area. I stared at the various climbing apparatuses and toys, wondering how the children who played here would react if a dragon landed in the field in broad daylight. They would probably be delighted and want to play with her, but I had no doubt mothers would have an apoplexy.

Leaving Lessie to rest, I made the short trek to the docks, only a few blocks from here. I knew the merchants would be coming in about now, carrying fish and livestock to sell to the local butchers, and if I bought from them directly, I could get a good deal on meat for Lessie.

Sure enough, a barge carrying sheep sailed into the dock just as I arrived, and I bought a medium-sized one off a farmer. I felt a bit bad as I tied a rope around his neck and led him back to Lessie, but there was nothing for it. If Lessie wasn't going to eat him, someone else would, and besides, I was no vegetarian myself.

"Oooh, fresh meat," Lessie said as I led the sheep into the garden. It let out a bleat of terror at the sight of my dragon, and I seized the rope with both hands as it immediately tried to bolt.

"I've got it," Lessie said, and I nearly jumped back as she lunged for the sheep. Within seconds, she had the animal in her jaws, and I winced as the bleating stopped instantly, replaced by the sound of crunching bones instead.

"Right." I took a step back and turned away to give her some privacy. Forget the mothers. The children would run screaming if they saw Lessie chomping on a whole sheep like this.

"I don't see what all the fuss is about," Lessie said with a huff.

"What does it matter if the sheep is whole or already skinned and cut into pieces? It's still a living creature."

I smiled wryly. *"I know. And I don't really have any issue with you hunting or eating animals. But I think any human would get a little nervous watching you go to town on something with those sharp teeth of yours."*

She flashed her bloody maw at me, exposing sharp, shiny teeth that seemed to be growing larger every day. *"That's the idea, isn't it?"*

Yep. It sure was. Having large, fire-breathing dragons who could devour a man whole had kept our country safe for centuries. But a dragon's fire was no match for cannon balls, and as Lessie ate, I felt a pang of sadness. She'd waited hundreds of years to be born only to arrive during a period when the time of dragons might very well come to an end.

"Not while I'm alive," Lessie said, curling her tail around my legs in a hug. *"Or the rest of us, for that matter. Muza is proof that dragons don't need to be enlisted in the Elantian army to live healthy, meaningful lives."*

I frowned at the note in her voice. *"Did Muza tell you what he does when he's not with Tavarian?"*

Lessie ducked her head, and if she'd been human, I was certain I'd see her blush. *"He told me a bit but said not to share with you. He said that it wasn't a secret for humans to know."*

I gritted my teeth at that, my blood simmering with annoyance. *"Tavarian knows,"* I said, but I knew that was different. Muza was his dragon, after all. And just because Lessie was mine didn't mean she had to share a secret she'd been entrusted with, unless it was a life-or-death thing. After all, she was her own person, so to speak.

Lessie finished the rest of her meal, then dropped me off on the rooftop of the Treasure Trove. My heart grew heavy with sadness as I watched her fly back to Dragon's Table, her form backlit by the moon hanging round and full in the air. I hoped Tavarian's negotiations with Quoronis were going well, and that he'd come back soon. Judging by what we'd seen across the border, I had a feeling we would be thrown into war much sooner than I'd anticipated.

10

"I think it might be time to give up."

"Already?" Carina arched her eyebrows, surprised at the defeated tone in my voice. We were in the back of the shop, taking advantage of an unexpected lull in customers to have lunch. "But you've only been searching for a few days, Zara. Zuar City is a big place."

"We've been searching almost a week," I said, kicking my legs out in front of me so I could cross them at the ankles. "Even with all the noise from the other objects in the city, we've covered quite a bit of territory. I'd think I would have come across something by now if Salcombe really was dumb enough to leave his piece of heart here. The more I think about it, the more unlikely it seems that he would have done that. At this point I'm just doing busy work, trying to pretend I'm doing something productive. If I had that journal, and those letters inside it, I could be tracking down that other piece of heart while Salcombe is still stuck in Zallabar."

Carina frowned, setting her half-eaten sandwich aside. "Maybe you should try tracking down Salcombe's associates. I was walking down Baker Street yesterday and I passed a few black-robed men. I shrugged them off as worshippers at first, but now that I think back, some of them might have been wearing that silver dragon emblem you were talking about."

"Worshippers?" I sat up straight, my mind whirling. "Are you talking about the Camatoz temple?"

"That's the one."

I chewed on my lip. Camatoz was a death deity that, like many of the old gods, had been widely worshipped by Elantians. The temple on Baker Street was a small relic left from that time, built right on top of one of the entrances to the old catacombs that wound beneath Zuar City. I'd visited both with Salcombe when I was a little girl, remembered his odd fascination with both the death god and the catacombs.

"Are you sure you didn't just see one of the temple priests?" I pressed. They wore black robes too.

"The temple priests don't have a dragon symbol on their robes," Carina insisted. "I'm sure it's them. They might be operating out of that same temple. In fact, I wouldn't be surprised if Salcombe hadn't recruited his acolytes from their ranks."

I mulled over that idea the rest of the day, and the more I thought about it, the more convinced I was that I needed to pay a visit. I itched to leave right away, but there was no point—the temple didn't open until dusk, when the last rays of light slipped away from the world. I always thought that was a bit strange—

after all, death came at all hours of the day—but then again, the temple was small. They probably didn't have enough staff to keep it open all the time.

The moment the clock struck seven, I was out of the chair and up the stairs. Carina gave me the side eye when I came down a few minutes later, wearing a black hooded cloak and a scarf that covered my distinctive red hair.

"Do you need me to come with you?" she asked.

I shook my head. "You've got stuff to do here, and besides, I'm familiar with the temple. I can handle myself."

She nodded. "Be careful, Zara. Salcombe might want you alive, but that doesn't mean his followers won't hurt you if they catch you."

Don't I know it, I thought, remembering Trolbos, Salcombe's henchman. I'd seen the looks the brute had given me when he thought no one was watching—if not for Salcombe, he'd have clubbed me over the head and dragged me off by the hair to have his way with me in some dark, scary place where I could scream myself hoarse and no one would be able to hear me. My fingers twitched, wishing for my dragon blade. But I had my daggers, and my wits, and that would have to be enough.

Climbing up the side of the building, I took to the rooftops. It was both safer and faster to travel here, away from the stench and riffraff of the city, and in twenty minutes, I was crouching over Baker Street, my eyes fixed on the temple just across the way.

Despite the negative connotations surrounding the death temple, it was a beautiful building. Two stories high, constructed of ebony and some kind of shiny black stone, it stood out next to the two brownstones flanking it not merely because of the materials it was constructed from, but also by the way it was shaped. The tall roof was steeply pitched, supported by pillars carved with vines, and over the entrance was a hooded figure with large, feathered wings that framed the double doors. All of this was illuminated by the lanterns that hung from the edge of the roof, each being painstakingly lit by a man with a hook as he shuffled around the perimeter.

For the next thirty minutes, I crouched in silence as I watched the temple. At first, I saw nothing unusual, just the comings and goings of parishioners attending the nightly service. Camatoz's following was small, just a few thousand people, but like most of the Elantians who still believed in the old gods, they were fervent worshippers. Many of them clutched offerings in their arms—bottles of wine, boxes filled with food, or precious objects—to entice the god into answering their prayers. Most of those prayers were benevolent—usually a wish to reconnect with a departed loved one, or to spare someone on their death bed. Some were more sinister, born of a desire for vengeance.

I wondered—if Camatoz was even real—whether the death god bothered to listen to his followers, to answer any of those prayers. Somehow, I didn't think so. I'd always thought of death as cold, uncaring, indiscriminate. When your time came, it came, and it didn't matter who you were, what good or bad you'd done in your life, or how much money you had.

In death's eyes, we were all equal.

My legs were just beginning to grow stiff when I saw five black-robed men approach the building. Casting my morbid thoughts aside, I focused my attention on them, and my breath caught as I noticed each of the men sported a flash of silver across their broad chests.

The dragon god's symbol.

Squinting, I leaned in to catch a glimpse of their faces, but the men wore silver masks to hide their identity. Damn. I was going to have to sneak inside the temple, find out where they were meeting. But how, without drawing attention to myself? For all I knew, the entire temple was under Salcombe's thumb, and they would seize me on the spot.

An idea began to form in the back of my mind, and I slunk away from the edge of the roof, taking care not to be seen. Quickly, I raced around the temple and across the city, heading for a manhole cover roughly a mile away. As a child, I'd been familiar with both the surface streets and the city's underbelly, and that knowledge was going to come in handy now.

After a quick look around to make sure no one was nearby, I dropped from the roof of the house I was currently perched on and approached the manhole cover. It came away with a hearty tug, and I wrinkled my nose as the familiar stench wafted up. The lovely aroma of sewage.

Yum.

Trying not to think too much about what I was getting into, I climbed down the grimy ladder, then hopped onto the tiny strip of land that served as a sidewalk. It was pitch dark down here, so I struck a match, then held it aloft with one hand to help me navigate my way through the warren of tunnels while I used the other to cover my nose and mouth.

Three matches later, I found the entrance to the catacombs. The heavy wooden door was secured with a lock, but the set of mundane lock picks I'd dug up from my apartment were more than good enough to get me through.

The moment I stepped inside, the call of thousands of valuable objects chimed in my mind. Closing the door, I turned the volume down, then lit another match so I could get my bearings. The catacombs stretched a good hundred miles beneath the city, and it was far too easy to get lost down here. Luckily, I had a pretty good sense of direction, and I'd used my treasure sense to fix the temple—and more importantly, the valuables inside it—in my mind's eye before I came down here.

Thankful for my spelled boots, I crept through the narrow corridors on silent feet, keeping my ears peeled for any activity. I didn't believe in ghosts, but I knew gangs and criminals often hid down here, and the last thing I wanted was to run into some asshole who thought I'd be an easy mark. If I could make my way into the temple without being seen, I might be able to eavesdrop on Salcombe's followers and learn some valuable information.

Aside from the threat of coming across thugs, my journey

through the catacombs was pleasant enough. The bodies buried in the walls had long turned to dust, so unlike the sewer tunnels, there was no stench. I'd come down here plenty of times as a desperate kid to filch tokens from the loculi—burial slots— carved into the walls, and in many ways it wasn't much different from any of the other ruins or sites I'd explored.

I was only a few blocks away from the temple when the sound of rhythmic chanting caught my attention. Frowning, I cocked my ear, at first thinking it might be coming from the temple. But the temple was too far away.

Could it be the dragon god cultists?

Drawn by the sound, I headed in the direction of the chanting, slowing my steps until I was standing outside a sepulcher—one of the many rooms in the catacombs that were dedicated to the burial of a specific family. Candlelight spilled into the corridor, making it impossible for me to peek through the doorway without being spotted, but thankfully one of the burial slots outside had a hole in the back that allowed me to peer straight into the large room without being seen.

Inside, the five robed men stood in a semi-circle, facing a large dragon statue mounted on the wall. It was carved of pure obsidian, with rubies set into its face for eyes, its maw opened wide as if it might scorch them all where they stood. In the center, on a small altar, was a large goblet filled with a clear liquid that shone like moonlight.

I focused my treasure sense on it, and a loud chime reverberated through my head, making me pause. There was something similar in the tone that reminded me of the dragon heart, and yet, the heart wasn't here.

The chanting swelled to a crescendo, drowning out the sound the goblet was making. Abruptly, they stopped, and the one standing closest to the dragon god's statue stepped forward. Pushing back his silver mask just enough to drink, he revealed full lips and a beard the color of autumn leaves.

The moment those lips touched the goblet, I sensed a ripple in the air, as if there had been a transfer of power. *That liquid,* I thought, staring at the cup as the man passed it off to the one on his left. *It must be infused with essence from the dragon heart!*

That explained how Salcombe was able to maintain his health even though he didn't have the heart on him. But I hadn't realized he was allowing his acolytes to reap the same benefits. Did that mean they had enhanced strength and health now, like he did? And how did imbibing such a substance affect their minds?

"Has there been any word from the master?" one of the cultists asked once they'd all finished partaking of the drink and their masks were firmly back in place. "What are our orders?"

"I have not had word from him since he crossed the Zallabarian border," the red-bearded man said. His voice was smooth and dark, like a fine red wine. "Until we do, we must continue to gather intelligence, and wait."

"I'm tired of waiting," another man groused. "We should be out there, helping him to recover the rest of the heart. Instead we are just sitting around, eavesdropping on conversations we're not allowed to do anything with. If he would allow us direct access to the heart—"

"That is not going to happen," Red Beard said, his harsh voice echoing off the dirt walls. "Our master trusted me alone with the location of the heart, so I could continue to harvest its essence and bring it to you. He has made it clear that under no circumstances are any of you allowed to touch the heart directly."

"And why is that?" one of the men asked. "Because the two of you are the only ones allowed to commune directly with the dragon god? How do we even know the god is real? Perhaps we should go back to worshipping Camatoz. At least *he* spoke to us."

Well that's new, I thought, leaning in. As I did, something skittered down my back, and I jumped, hitting my head on the top of the burial slot.

Instantly, the room went silent. "What was that?" Red Beard barked.

Shit.

I didn't wait for the men to come out and investigate. Digging a smoke bomb from my pouch, I lit it, then tossed it into the sepulcher as I raced past. Their shouts echoed in the hall as I sprinted back the way I came, knowing there was no way I'd make it through the temple without getting caught. The conversation I'd overheard had made it clear some of these men used to be Camatoz's followers, and who knew what kind of relationship the priests had with the dragon god's acolytes?

I dodged to the side at the sound of a blade zipping through the air, but it sliced the side of my thigh anyway. Crying out, I stumbled against the wall, then gritted my teeth and pushed through the pain.

"You're not getting away!" one of the cultists roared, rushing out from another corridor that intersected with mine. He was huge. Terror gripped me as he raised his sword above his head with two hands, and I barely managed to flatten my back against the wall before he swung it down. Darting in close, I slashed the side of his neck with my dagger. Blood spurted from the wound, splashing me in the face as he screamed, and I quickly darted around him as he clutched at the gash. The sound of rapidly approaching footsteps spurred me on, but I had the advantage of silent feet, and eventually I managed to lose them.

Panting hard, I sprinted back through the sewer passages and climbed up the ladder as fast as I could. Relief surged through me as I shoved the manhole cover away, and I climbed up—

Only to be seized by two guards.

"Zara Kenrook." A third guard smiled smugly. "Fancy seeing you here."

I glared at the muncie, who I recognized from previous run-ins. "Clancy," I spat as I struggled against the guards. "This is a mistake. You have to let me go!"

"A mistake?" Clancy arched his eyebrows. "If you mean breaking the law is a mistake, then you're right. Going down into the catacombs without a permit is illegal, Zara. You know that."

"I wasn't going down there to steal!" I hissed. "I was tracking a group of cultists!"

"I don't care if you were down there on your knees, giving blow jobs to the chancellor himself," Clancy said as the other two muncies slapped restraints on my wrists. "You're under arrest for trespassing on government property."

11

I spent the night on a hard cot in a jail cell, staring up at the ceiling and wracking my brain. The muncies had confiscated my lock picks, so there was no getting out, and lying around here while those cultists were on the street was driving me nuts. I needed to be out there, tracking down Red Beard so I could squeeze him for details. He was the only one, aside from Salcombe, who knew where that piece of heart was.

Unfortunately, the muncies had been entirely unsympathetic to my cause. The captain of the guard laughed in my face when I told him about the dragon god and the cultists, and invoking Captain Marcas's name hadn't helped. "I've already contacted the upper city guard," he'd sneered through the bars at me. "I'm sure someone will be along to take you back to your cushy new life."

Lessie had been beside herself when she'd come to meet me for our nightly flight and found me missing. I'd been tempted to let her storm the walls of the jail just to see the look on the muncies' faces, but I knew I was already in big trouble. If they really had sent word to the upper city that I was here, then the headmaster would soon find out that I wasn't at Tavarian's hidden estate anymore.

Eventually, I managed to doze off just as the early grey light of dawn poked its fingers through the tiny window in my cell. But it seemed like I'd just closed my eyes when I heard boots clopping down the hall, voices in conversation.

"Yes, yes, open the door," a woman ordered impatiently. I opened my eyes at the familiar voice, then sat up abruptly at the sight of Major Falkieth standing outside.

"Major!" Heat stung my cheeks as I jumped to attention. "I—I didn't think—"

"That I would come get you myself?" she barked. Her steely eyes raked over my disheveled appearance, disapproval in every line of her hard face. "The headmaster received a report that you were spotted flying over Dragon's Table and sent me down here to fetch you. I refused to believe you would be hiding out here, given the severity of your circumstances, but I see now that the report was correct. I am very disappointed in you."

Anger sparked in my chest, warring with my embarrassment. "I wasn't 'hiding out' here. Lessie and I have been scouring the city, looking for Salcombe's piece of the dragon god's heart. I was following a group of Salcombe's followers tonight, and I heard—"

"I don't care what you were doing," she interrupted. "Mr. Lyton told us that he and Miss Thomas"—that was Jallis and Rhia

—"escorted you back to Tavarian's home, and that is where you should have gone. Since you did not, you must return to the academy at once. How can you even think of shirking your duty now, when war is upon us?"

"What?" Chills raced down my spine. "We're being called to the battlefront too?"

"Many of the older cadets will be called to fight, certainly," Falkieth said. "You and your dragon are a bit young for combat, but the generals may find a use for you. With Zallabar threatening war every day, we must all be prepared for the coming conflict."

I shook my head. "This is happening far too quickly."

To my surprise, I caught a flicker of sympathy in Falkieth's eyes. "Be that as it may, you must still answer the call." She shoved up from her chair. "I'll escort you back to your old home so you can pack your things. You have three hours to report back to the academy."

"Thank you." I wanted to beg for more time, so I could follow up on my lead, but the tone in Falkieth's voice brooked no argument. "Any chance you could help me get my belongings back from the guards before I go?" I ventured.

Major Falkieth raised her eyebrows. "You mean these?" she asked, pulling out my lock picks and knives from her satchel.

"Yes!" I had to stop myself from snatching hem out of her hands.

"I'm not certain I approve of the lock picks," she said dryly. "But take them and go, before I change my mind."

She didn't have to tell me twice.

Back at the shop, Carina and Kira descended upon me like hawks. "What happened to you?" Carina cried, taking in the blood on my pants.

"A close call from one of the cultists." I waved a hand. "It's not a big deal." The muncies had applied some basic first aid, stitching and bandages. I'd have a scar, but no lasting damage. "I ended up finding them in the catacombs."

There was a lull in customers, so we left Kira and Nate to watch the front of the shop while I went upstairs to pack and explain to Carina what had happened. By the time I was finished, she was pale as a ghost.

"War?" Carina asked. "Zara, they're not really expecting you and Lessie to serve so soon, are they?"

"I'm a dragon rider," I said. "All riders are automatically conscripted into the Elantian army for ten years. If the military decides that they need us, we'll have to go. Lessie is a female dragon," I added at the stricken look on her face, "and still young, so it's doubtful that we'll be put on the front lines. I'm hoping we won't be called at all, but if we are, it'll probably be for some smaller task, like reconnaissance."

"Spying," Carina exclaimed. "That's even more dangerous!"

"As I said, that's only *if* we're called. But either way, I have to go."

Zipping up my bag, I stood, then slung it over my shoulder. Carina immediately threw her arms around me, wrapping me up in a bone-crushing hug. "You'd better tell me if they send you off somewhere," she said fiercely. "And write me every chance you get."

"I will," I promised, returning the hug while I fought back tears. If I cried now, Carina would fall apart, and I needed her to stay strong. She had to keep things running while I was gone, if not for us, then for all the orphans we employed. The boys and girls who'd been given a chance at a better life, thanks to our good fortune and hard work.

Swallowing hard, I left.

As I rode up the elevators to Dragon's Table, I reached out to Lessie. *"Has anyone come looking for you?"*

"Yes," she said, sounding grumpy. *"Major Falkieth showed up with her dragon to escort me back. I'm at the stables now."*

Alarmed, I reached through the bond to get a better sense of how she was feeling. *"Is everything okay? Are you hurt?"*

"Fine," she said. *"But they woke me up from a very nice nap, and Odorath was rather rude. He seems to think that just because he is older than me, he has the right to scold me as if he were my mother."*

I snorted. *"Most cultures and societies teach you to respect and listen to your elders,"* I pointed out.

"Elders," she huffed. *"I wonder whose dragon egg was laid first, mine or his?"*

Shaking my head, I stepped off the elevator and hired a cab to take me the rest of the way to Dragon Rider Academy. The two-story brick estate with its manicured gardens was exactly the way I remembered it, and to my surprise, I felt a sense of home-coming as I approached.

The guards manning the entrance seemed to be expecting me and told me to report to the headmaster. I went up to the second floor, where the secretary promptly sat me down in one of the visitor's chairs in the hallway outside the headmaster's office to cool my heels. Still tired from having been up all night, I leaned my head back against the wall and started to doze off, ignoring the woman's glare.

"Hey." Jallis's voice tugged me from my nap, his shoulder brushing mine as he sat in the chair next to me. "You okay?"

I opened my eyes, and he smiled. "It's too early in the morning for you to be this cheerful," I grumbled.

He raised an eyebrow and glanced at the clock. Nearly noon. "I'm guessing you didn't get much sleep last night?"

"No." I lowered my voice to a whisper, in case anyone was listening. "I was out looking for the heart."

"Yeah, I figured that's what you were doing when Kadryn told me you flew over Dragon's Table last night," Jallis said. "Did you and Lessie find anything? Why were you down in the catacombs?"

"We were running out of places to look," I told him. I debated whether or not to tell him about the cultists, but decided against it. Really, what was Jallis going to be able to do? "But it doesn't matter now. I'm back here."

Jallis's mouth softened in sympathy as he picked up on the note of misery in my voice. "The headmaster isn't going to punish you or Lessie, Zara. He knows that Lord Tavarian is in Quoronis and you weren't trying to desert. He didn't even give Rhia or me demerits, even though we left without telling anyone, just a warning. I'm sure he's just happy that you're back safe after Salcombe kidnapped you. You're still a cadet, Zara, which means that he and Tavarian are responsible for your safety."

"Huh." I didn't really think about it, but if I were in their shoes, I would feel bad about letting me get kidnapped on their watch. "So, he knows Tavarian is in Quoronis?"

"Yes, although nobody has any idea if he's made any progress with them." Jallis's lips twisted into a grimace. "I did tell the headmaster about the cannons, and he had me give a full report to the council, but I still don't think they grasp the severity of the situation."

"Lord Tavarian would," I said with a sigh. "I wish he was back already. If Quoronis isn't going to back down, then we need him more than ever so the council and the generals fully understand what we're up against. The last thing we need to be doing is rushing into battle unprepared."

"Speaking of rushing into battle," Jallis said, "all the third-year cadets have been told to report to the forward camp near the Zallabarian border. Kadryn and I will be leaving tonight."

"Tonight?" I twisted fully in my chair to face him. "But...but I just got back. I've barely had a chance to spend two minutes with you since you and Rhia rescued me from Salcombe's ship."

"I know." He gave me a rueful smile and reached up to touch the side of my face. "That's why I sought you out now. I wanted to catch up, and I wanted to say goodbye."

The warmth of his hand sank into my skin, drawing me closer to him. Footsteps came down the hall toward us—probably another passing student—but if Jallis noticed, he didn't care. He simply drew me to him and pressed his mouth against mine in a slow, tender kiss.

Tears sprang to my eyes as I wrapped my arms around his neck and kissed him back. This wasn't fair. None of it was. I wasn't sure what, exactly, Jallis and I had together, but I liked him and wanted to explore it. How would I have the chance to do that if he ended up maimed or killed? And what about Kadryn? Jallis's dragon wasn't a youngling like Lessie, but he was still only a few years old. I couldn't bear the thought of him, or Lessie, or any dragon being shredded by cannon fire.

But that was the reality of war. Regardless of whether or not we'd provoked or bullied Zallabar into attacking us, we still needed to protect our land and our people. We would do what we must. Even if that meant sending these precious, rare creatures out to fight our battles.

Jallis stroked a hand down my back as he kissed me, sensing my grief and anger. The firm, comforting touch alleviated some of the turmoil in my heart, and I leaned into the kiss. The warmth his touch kindled inside me quickly began to burn hotter, and the kiss grew fiercer. It would be so easy to take his hand and tug him down the hallway, find an empty closet, and see just what else he could do with those hands—

"Miss Kenrook—" the headmaster began as the door opened, and then he made a strangled sound. "Mr. Lyton! What is the meaning of this?"

We flew apart, my cheeks burning crimson. Jallis's face was rather red, too, but he covered up his embarrassment with a disarming grin.

"Sorry, headmaster. Just saying goodbye to my girl before I get sent off to the trenches." He leaned in and pressed another kiss to my lips, though this one was far more chaste. "Don't worry," he murmured against my mouth. "Everything is going to be fine."

I clung to those words, wanting to believe they were true, as I followed the headmaster into his office. Even if, in my heart, I knew he was wrong.

12

When I entered the mess hall the next morning, all heads turned to look at me.

I paused at the entrance for half a heartbeat, taking everyone in. Normally, the mess hall was a cheerful place, where cadets laughed and talked and bonded before and between classes, but today the mood was somber. Grim. The threat of war hung over our heads, and it showed in the faces of my fellow cadets. Shadows dogged their eyes, lines bracketed their mouths, and tension crackled in the air, so potent I almost believed it could ignite a powder keg and blow us all to smithereens, if someone brought said keg in here.

At least that will save the Zallabarians the effort of having to kill us, I thought sourly.

The moment passed, and I strode into the room, ignoring the stares. I was notorious around here for many reasons, chief among them having grown up in the lower city, away from dragon rider society. No one knew which dragon rider family I'd descended from, since I'd been orphaned, and I hadn't even known I *was* a rider until a few months ago, when I'd broken into Tavarian's house to try to steal the piece of heart he had hidden. Instead, I found what looked like a petrified dragon egg, and when I touched it, the dragon inside came to life and called to my soul.

Despite all the crap I'd had to deal with since becoming a rider, I didn't regret touching that dragon egg. Not one iota. I would face down the dragon god himself if he tried to come between Lessie and me—she was as much a part of me as my beating heart, and the thought of being separated even for an instant was enough to make my gut twist in misery.

Lessie's consciousness rubbed against my own, a silent, reassuring touch, and I smiled despite the grim mood in the room. No matter what happened, even if we did get thrown into this stupid war, at least the two of us would have each other. The bond that tied us together ensured that we were never truly separated, even if we were miles apart.

"Hey," Rhia said as I sat down across from her. My breakfast tray was loaded with eggs, toast, and oatmeal, and I immediately tucked in. "You sleep okay?"

"As well as anyone else in this place," I said with a shrug. "You?"

Rhia grinned. "Like a log. Major Falkieth worked us hard yesterday, so Ykos and I were both exhausted."

"I bet." My shoulders tightened with tension. "She introduce any new drills?"

"Mostly evasive maneuvers for us first-years," Rhia said. "Although I heard a rumor we might start stealth training soon."

"Stealth training?"

"Learning how to stay hidden in the sky, day or night," another cadet said, his brown eyes sparkling with excitement. "I think it'll mostly be night flying, though. Word is they want to use us for reconnaissance and possibly carrying messages."

I let out a sigh of relief. "I had a feeling that might be the case." Even though I wasn't happy about getting pulled into the war at all, at least the academy was going to give us proper training. All that night flying Lessie and I had been doing was about to come in handy.

"I don't know why everyone is so gloomy," another cadet, this one a second-year named Kade, said with a scoff. "So what if the Zallabarians have a few cannons? We should still be able to outmaneuver them. Our dragons are fast, and they breathe fire. What do you think happens if you breathe fire onto a barrel of gunpowder?"

"It explodes!" another cadet crowed, and the crowd rippled with laughter.

"You're idiots," I snapped, anger heating my blood at their lack-adaisical attitude. The room grew quiet as eyes turned to me, but I stood up rather than shrinking away, refusing to back down. "Rhia and I saw those cannons up close, and her dragon, Ykos, got a taste of what the shrapnel bombs could do. They're going to have more cannons than we have dragons, and for all you know, they might have other weapons that we don't even know about."

"So what?" Kade sneered. "Are we supposed to just sit here and cower in our beds because of what the Zallabarians *might* be able to do to us? We're dragon riders. We fear no one."

Cheers rose from the crowd, but I raked them all with a scathing look. "Look at you all. So eager to rush into battle. How many in this room have dragons?"

The room fell silent again as eight people slowly raised their hands. I shook my head in disgust. "Eight. The rest of you have no idea what it's like to bond with a dragon, to share your soul with such a magnificent creature, and yet you're so happy to send us all off into battle. Some of you will eventually become lieutenants and captains, maybe even generals someday, ordering us into battle. Perhaps, before you get there, you might want to think about how to *save* lives, not just how to take them."

I snatched up my tray and stormed out of the mess hall, still fuming. Whispers trailed in my wake, and a couple of the cadets scoffed and snickered, but as I left, the whispers turned to worried buzzing. Good. Maybe I'd given these jerks something to think about.

I finished the rest of my breakfast in the garden, then reviewed the new schedule. All normal classes had been canceled;

instead, we'd be dividing our time between the greenhouse, the blacksmith, and the training fields, preparing for war.

The next couple of days passed in a blur of activity. All of us were assigned to different professors to help with the war effort. I spent half my mornings with the herbology professor, mixing up poultices and potions to be sent to the camps, and the other half with the blacksmith, helping him at the forge as he crafted and repaired weapons and armor. In the afternoons, we were all out on the field with Major Falkieth, who put us through our paces, along with two other drill instructors.

"Very good," Major Falkieth said in my headpiece as Lessie and I successfully executed a barrel roll together. "Lord Tavarian has been training you well."

"Thank you," I said, feeling a pang in my heart even as my chest swelled with pride. I'd been worried Major Falkieth was still angry with me, but she seemed to have put my transgression behind her. Even so, her words reminded me of my missing benefactor, and my mood sank. Was Tavarian ever going to come back? Of the three countries we were about to go to war with, Quoronis was by far the most civilized, but that didn't mean Tavarian was completely safe. I wished he'd gone with an escort, even if he did have magic to protect himself with. There was only so much one man could do against the might of a nation.

As we moved into the second week of training, Major Falkieth did indeed start us on stealth training, as Rhia had predicted. "You'll each be given a specific building on Dragon's Table to seek out," Major Falkieth said as she paced back and forth in front of us. A cadet came down the line with a box, and we each reached in and grabbed a piece of paper. "Your task is to fly to that building, jot down as many details about it as possible, and then return, all without being spotted by the city guards. They are on alert to expect you, so don't think this is going to be easy."

"But Major Falkieth," one of the cadets complained, "how are we supposed to see anything when there's no moon out, and we'll be so far away?"

Major Falkieth grinned, hoisting up a leather sack that had been sitting nearby on the ground. "With these."

She opened up the bag and walked down the line, handing each of us a pair of goggles. My heart rose in excitement as she pressed one into my hand—I'd been missing the goggles that Carina had given me, which I'd left back at Tavarian's along with every other valuable I owned. They didn't have the same dials and knobs that my other ones did, but my treasure sense told me that they were valuable, and magical in nature.

"These are special night-vision goggles," Falkieth shouted as she came to stand in front of us again. She held up her own pair for us to see, the torchlight flickering across her face. "When you put them on, you'll notice a green haze come over your vision, but that's normal. They are enchanted to be unbreakable, but I wouldn't drop them if I were you. I think you'll find it a lot harder to remain undetected if you have to swoop to the ground to retrieve them."

Nervous laughter rippled through the crowd as we all put the goggles on. As Falkieth had said, a green haze immediately covered my vision, but suddenly I was able to make out details the torches hadn't been able to illuminate. I could see the academy building and the stables clearly now, and as I swept my gaze across the field, I caught the rustle of grass as a rodent scampered away.

"They don't zoom in like my other ones do," I said ruefully to Lessie, who was lined up with the other dragons behind me. She had grown almost fifty percent larger since we arrived—the stable masters were practically force-feeding her, and her body, eager to catch up after being stuck in that egg for so long, happily gobbled up all the energy. When she wasn't out training with me, she slept, her body using that food to grow her muscles and tendons.

"That doesn't matter," she said. *"I have excellent night vision."*

"This is one of those exercises where the bond between dragon and rider becomes even more important," Major Falkieth said, almost as if she'd read my mind. "Your dragons have fantastic vision, day and night, and can see things from far distances that you and I cannot. While you may not be able to make out certain details from a distance, they will, so use that. The more detailed your descriptions are, the more points you will get."

With that, Lessie and I mounted up, and we all flew into the night sky. Ironically, the building we'd been given was Barrigan's Antiques, the shop of the antiquities collector I used to work with who'd been trying to drive me out of business. I wondered what he'd think if he could see Lessie and me now, flying over his building.

"Here we are," Lessie said, hovering above the building. She'd positioned herself far enough away that the guards on the ground would not be able to see her, and now that her wings had grown stronger, she was able to hold herself more steadily in one position. *"You have your pen and paper?"*

"Yep."

I whipped out my notepad, and between the two of us, filled several pages with notes. In addition to the basic decorative details about the building, I jotted down the number of windows, exits, and entrances, how many guards were in the area, and other important details, asking Lessie questions to help clarify things with her superior sight. As someone who used to break into places like this for a living, it was practically second nature, and the night-vision goggles as well as Lessie's sight made the job even easier. In no time, we turned around and headed back to the field.

Major Falkieth was very impressed with my notes, and the following nights she made sure to give Lessie and me tasks that were slightly more difficult than the others'. On more than one occasion, she and the drill sergeants looked at Lessie as they talked, which made me uneasy. Were they singling us out for a particular task?

Lessie, of course, was thrilled about it. *"Of course they are going to give us a mission,"* she said, puffing her chest out with pride. *"I may be small, but I am much faster than these other dragons, and you have the eyes and brains for this sort of work."*

"That's not reassuring," I grumbled.

She flicked her tongue out, her fiery gaze sparking with annoyance. *"I know that you don't want to be involved in the war, Zara, but since we have no choice, we may as well make ourselves useful. Perhaps you do not care either way, but my pride will not allow me to be relegated to the bench when so many lives are at stake."*

"I don't mind benches," I shot back, stung and a little surprised by the dig. I didn't think Lessie had it in her to be catty toward me, but I guess I shouldn't be surprised. She was sassy to everyone else, after all. *"They're sturdy, supportive, and they don't generally put you in the line of fire."*

The next night, Major Falkieth changed things up a bit. "Tonight, you are going to work in pairs," she announced, the wind whipping her steel-colored braid through the air. A storm was brewing in the air, and I shivered a little as the chill blew straight through my riding leathers. "Earlier tonight, we hid a series of boxes in Briarwood Forest. Each box has a symbol on it, four boxes per symbol, twenty boxes total. Your objective is to retrieve your boxes only and return with them to base within two hours. Those who fail to complete the task within the allotted time will be mucking out stalls tomorrow."

Groans went up from the other cadets, but I stifled a grin as I felt a surge of excitement from Lessie. They might only be boxes, but this was a treasure hunt, and as such, I had a distinct advantage.

To our mutual delight, Major Falkieth paired Rhia and me up. "This is going to be so fun," she gushed as we studied the symbol we were given—an eight-pointed cross.

"Mount up!" Major Falkieth shouted. "Your time is about to start!"

Hurriedly, we scrambled up our dragons and into the saddles. Major Falkieth blew her whistle, the shrill sound echoing in the night, and all ten dragons launched into the air, heading for the forest.

Briarwood Forest was roughly half an hour's flight from Zuar City, a small patch of sparsely wooded forest split down the middle by a minor river. The stinging cold was even worse up here, and I ducked my head as icy drizzle began to spatter my cheeks. I was certain Major Falkieth had deliberately picked a night with bad weather—after all, riders didn't have the luxury of waiting for clear skies to do battle. We were expected to perform in all kinds of weather.

"Here we go," Lessie said, coming in low. She twisted to the side to maneuver through a narrow space between the trees, and I squeezed my legs against her sides as I gripped the pommel, clinging tight. *"Do you sense anything?"*

I opened up my treasure sense, straining to focus in on the boxes. This was a bit more difficult, as the boxes didn't have significant value like most treasure did, and there were real valuables buried beneath the forest floor that the treasure hunter in me itched to dig up. *"This way,"* I said, sensing something to our left. *"Tell Ykos so he can follow."*

I gave Lessie a mental sense of where I felt the box was, and she veered in that direction, careful not to scrape her wings against the tree branches. The trees were far enough apart that the other dragons could navigate as well, but despite Lessie's recent growth spurt, she was still smaller, and could navigate the turns much easier and faster.

"Here we go," I said as I spotted a box hanging from a tree branch. They'd been tied to the branches, which was smart, because the winds were strong enough that they all would have blown away by now. *"Slow down just a hair."*

Lessie did as I asked, and I reached out and snatched the box up. *"Dammit,"* I cursed as I held it up to my night vision to inspect the symbol. *"Wrong one."*

Lessie circled back around so I could return the box to the tree branch, wasting precious time. I scowled at the sound of someone else crowing triumphantly, and Lessie huffed, echoing my sentiment.

"Maybe we should try splitting up," Rhia shouted over the wind as she passed me. "We'll get more done if we can divide and conquer."

"Yeah, okay," I shouted back. Pulling up the mental map in my head, I marked the locations of where I thought the boxes closest to us were, and then sent that image to Lessie. *"Tell Ykos to take the ones on the right,"* I told her. *"We'll go left."*

Once we did that, the hunt became much easier. After two more duds, Lessie and I finally grabbed a box, and so did Rhia.

"Two down, two to go," I told Lessie. *"And then we can get out of this blistering cold."*

Lessie made a low sound of agreement. *"The weather is miserable,"* she said, *"but at least we're together, and you're not still stuck with Salcombe—"*

An explosion rattled my teeth, and Lessie immediately ducked lower, her belly nearly scraping the ground. The hairs on my arms rose, my neck prickling with dread—I knew that sound. A shrapnel cannon, disturbingly close even though we were nowhere near the Zallabarian border.

"Get some altitude," I ordered Lessie. *"Tell Ykos to follow."*

Lessie flapped her wings hard, pushing us high into the sky, above the burgeoning clouds. Rhia followed suit, and the two of us exchanged worried glances as we moved away from where we'd heard the sound, using the clouds for cover.

"I don't understand what's going on," Rhia shouted above the roaring winds. "How can there be cannons here? Has the war already started?"

"I don't know, but we need to warn the others!" I shouted back. Through the bond, I could feel Lessie's anxiousness as she reached out to the other dragons, warning them to take their riders to safety. We needed to get back to the academy, to tell Major Falkieth what was going on—

The pained roar of a dragon ripped through my thoughts, and Lessie jerked, nearly tossing me from the saddle. *"It's Ragor!"* she cried. *"He's hurt!"*

"Shit." Ragor was Ullion Tegar's dragon, a second-year rider and a fresh-faced seventeen-year-old with a gentle soul. Anger bloomed in my chest at the thought of him or his dragon hurt— he had no business getting caught up in a war like this. *"How bad is it?"*

"A large gash in his side," Lessie said. *"He's in too much pain to fly his rider back to the academy, so he's seeking shelter in the trees."*

I gritted my teeth. *"We need to figure out where this cannon fire is coming from."*

Using Lessie, I silently communicated to Ykos and Rhia to stay quiet and follow me. Carefully, the four of us flew higher, scanning the skies for anything out of place. As we rose above another layer of clouds, Lessie stopped short just before we crashed into a large, dark object, and my heart flew into my throat.

"Dragon's balls!"

"What IS *that?"* Lessie asked, hastily backpedaling away. But before she could get very far, I squeezed my legs, commanding her to stay where she was.

"It's the hull of an airship." Swallowing hard, I craned my neck to get a better look. We'd been directly beneath the belly, and now that Lessie had moved back a bit, I could see the cannons sticking out from the aft side. Two in total, and probably two more on the other side.

Rhia and her dragon rose from the clouds on my left side, and her eyes nearly bugged out of her skull at the sight of the warship. Pressing my fingers to my lips, I used my dragon to communicate with her, not wanting to risk being overheard. We were damned lucky the crew didn't seem to notice us hovering below, and I wanted to take full advantage of the element of surprise.

The sound of something crackling made my skin prickle, and I clapped my hands to my ears. *"Get down!"* I mentally shouted at Lessie.

Lessie and Ykos both dropped beneath the cloud layer just as the ship fired another cannon. My heart pounded hard, blood thrumming in my ears as I wondered if another dragon had been hit. Poking up above the clouds, this time on the other side, I was surprised there were no cannons.

"Rhia suspects that more would have weighed the ship down too much," Lessie relayed after I'd told them what we'd seen.

"Right." We regrouped below the clouds. "We need to take out that ship," I shouted at Rhia.

"Should we try jamming the cannons first?" Rhia shouted back.

I shook my head. "Too risky. Besides, if we destroy the cannons, we'll never be able to get a chance to study them properly."

The two of us briefly conferred, then flew around to the port side of the ship. Rising through the clouds, our dragons opened their mouths and immediately began blasting the airship with fire. Screams filled the air as the flames licked the sides of the ship, but the moisture from the atmosphere protected it, keeping the fire from spreading as rapidly as we would have liked.

"Go for the air balloon!" I shouted at Rhia.

Ykos flapped his wings, pushing him and Rhia higher into the air as the crew began shooting at us. Lessie roared as one of the bolts grazed her wing, but the danger only spurred her on. We darted around the ship, evading more bolts as we continued to bombard the crew with fire. One of Lessie's fireballs made it past the men guarding the cannons and collided with a pile of shrapnel bombs.

"Duck!" I screamed, and Lessie dropped like a stone, so fast that my ass briefly left the saddle before being yanked back down by the stirrups. I clapped my hands over my ears, but the resulting explosion still rattled my brain.

"They did it!" Lessie crowed as Rhia and Ykos sped away from the ship. Sure enough, I saw that the giant balloon holding it airborne had been destroyed. Lessie and I hurriedly got clear of the ship as it immediately began to plummet to the ground, trailing smoke and screams in its wake.

The dragons roared their triumph to the sky, lighting up the clouds with more streams of fire, and Rhia and I exchanged grins. Her face was flushed, her thick chestnut hair flying like a wild cloud around her head, and her eyes blazed with the same thrill of victory I was feeling.

But that heady feeling quickly disappeared as I looked down and remembered the injured dragon. Sensing my thoughts, Lessie tucked her wings in at her sides, and we dove through the layers of clouds, heading back to the forest to search for our fallen comrade. As the ground finally came into view again, we saw smoke rising from the field—the ship had crash-landed just on the outskirts of the forest, quickly becoming a blaze of kindling.

"I doubt any of them survived that," Lessie said.

Flying lower, we passed over the ship briefly to check if there were any survivors. Seeing none, we continued over the forest until we found Ragor and Ullion. My gut twisted as we flew over splintered trees that had been hit by the cannons—several were on fire, and Lessie used the gusts from her wings to put them out as we passed. Ullion and his dragon were huddled under a large tree that remained unscathed, and I winced at the sight—the dragon had spread his left wing out on the ground, and it was torn and bleeding in multiple places. Ullion was curled up against his dragon's other side, clutching his leg, which was also soaked in blood.

Lessie landed a few feet away, and I jumped to the ground and ran over to them. "What happened?" I asked as I dropped to Ullion's side. "Where's your partner?"

"I-I'm not sure," Ullion stammered, his voice shaky. The boy's face was pale with blood loss, and anger surged through me that his partner wasn't here with him. "I think he fled with everyone else."

Rhia sighed as she approached, a sympathetic expression on her face. "You can't blame him, Zara," she said, putting a hand on my shoulder. "We did tell all of them to run."

"Sure, but I wouldn't have left you," I growled.

"Nor I, you," Rhia agreed. "But most of these guys are still kids."

I looked at Ullion again. His freckled face was baby smooth, his eyes glazed over with shock, and I had to agree with Rhia. He was a kid, as were so many of the other cadets. Raised in luxury, with no real concept of war since it had been so long since Elantia had been involved in any real conflict. Most of the wars we'd been involved in happened in foreign territory; few countries were brave enough to attack us on our home turf.

A quick examination of Ullion's wound told me that he still had shrapnel embedded in his leg and would need surgery from a doctor or mage healer. I drew my knife and cut off a piece of his tunic to bind the wound, then handed him off to Rhia to take him back to the academy. Lessie and I would wait here with Ragor, who was still bleeding and defenseless, until someone could come out to heal him, too.

While Lessie licked the blood from Ragor's wounds, trying to close them up, another dragon landed in the clearing. I narrowed my eyes as another boy, this one even younger than Ullion, dismounted and approached. Kade Malte, I thought, digging his name up.

"W-where's Ullion?" Kade asked, his eyes darting around the small clearing.

"Heading back to the academy." I pushed myself to my feet despite the exhaustion dragging at my limbs. "You're his partner?"

"Yeah." He looked at Ragor's shredded wing, guilt written all over his pale face. "I wanted to help him, but I was too scared to approach. The sound of that cannon fire—"

"It's all right," I said, gentling my voice. The fear and guilt eating at him eroded my anger, and I let out a deep sigh. "You did the right thing, hanging back until the cannon fire stopped, and then coming back to find your partner."

He nodded shakily. "Should I go back to the academy and check on him? Or do you need help watching his dragon? Gosh, that looks like an awful wound," he said, peering around me at Ragor again.

Ragor made a grumbling sound in his throat, as if in agreement. "I think you should stick around a bit," I told him, eyeing the sword strapped to his side. "It'll be nice to have another dragon to help protect Ragor while we wait for help, and you can be my backup."

"Your backup? For what?"

I gave him a tight grin. "We're going to go exploring."

Leaving Lessie, Ragor, and Dinmar—the third dragon—behind to help with Ragor's wounds, Kade and I set out for the airship. We walked a good forty minutes to reach the edge of the forest, but the downed airship was easy enough to find, still spewing smoke into the sky. The stench of charred flesh, wood, and gunpowder reached my nose long before we stepped out of the woods, and Kade retched a little.

"This is terrible," he said as we circled the wreckage. The remnants of the cannons were strewn about the grass, and he kicked at one of the smoking pieces of metal. "This thing did so much damage, and that was just one ship. What if we'd had to face off against a dozen?"

"That's what I've been saying," I said grimly as I poked through the remains of the airship. One of the cannons was damaged beyond repair, but the other one was merely cracked—still salvageable, and certainly intact enough for us to study. The cabin had broken into several pieces, and I counted the scorched bodies of seven men in the grass. "The enemy has vastly superior technology to us, and the capability to hurt our dragons badly."

Kade nodded. "You were right, Zara," he said. "When you told us in the mess hall that we were too cocky, and that Zallabar had superior weapons, I thought you were exaggerating. But this..." He shook his head. "It's monstrous."

I nodded, crouching in the grass to examine one of the bodies. I felt no pleasure in his acknowledgment—I'd rather Ragor and Ullion be whole and healthy over the Zallabarians proving me right about my fears. I studied the man's clothing. He wore plain leathers rather than a military uniform. Were these men undercover, or were they mercenaries?

"If Zallabar is swelling their ranks with soldiers for hire, we are in bigger trouble than we thought," Lessie said.

"No kidding." I straightened, turning to look at Kade. "Do you see anything about this ship that identifies it as Zallabarian?"

Kade pursed his lips a minute as he scanned the wreckage, then shook his head. "Nothing. The men aren't wearing uniforms, and there are no identifying markings on the canvas or the ship itself. If not for the cannons, there'd be no way of knowing."

I nodded my agreement. "What do you think they were doing here?"

Kade turned south, looking back toward the city. "If I had to guess, I'd say they were on their way to Dragon's Table," he said. "Maybe they planned to hit the stables and try to scare our dragons out into the open so they could maim and kill them before we were called to active duty."

"Except they didn't have to," I said grimly, "because we were already out here, flying about without a care and ripe for the picking."

Rage burned in my gut as I thought of how the Zallabarians must have gleefully turned their ship toward the forest. It should have been perfectly safe for these cadets to fly within our own territory; Zuar City was nowhere near the border. With no one patrolling the skies this far up, they had managed to sneak a ship into our airspace and target our precious dragons. It was unacceptable.

"How did the airship end up down here?" Kade asked.

"Rhia and I found it high up in the clouds," I told him. "It hadn't noticed us, so we came around from behind and torched it."

"That's crazy," Kade said, shaking his head. "Crazy, and amazing. Thank you." He bowed his head. "You probably saved my partner's life tonight."

The sound of flapping wings drew our attention to the sky, and we turned to see Major Falkieth and Headmaster Caparro descending, along with five other riders. "Son of a hoggleswaith," Major Falkieth swore as she rushed over to the smoldering remains of the airship. "So, it's true!"

The headmaster was on her heels, his eyes wide with disbelief as he took in the scene. "Where is the injured dragon?" he demanded.

"Farther into the woods," I told him. "I can lead you there—"

"I'll do it," Kade interrupted, stepping forward. He turned toward the two riders standing nearby and holding medical supplies. "Follow me."

He strode back into the forest, and the other riders followed, leaving me alone with Falkieth and Caparro. Taking a deep breath, I steeled myself for their questions, and gave them my full report.

When I was finished, the headmaster shook his head. "What you and Rhia did tonight was a bit foolish, but very brave. The two of you, and your dragons, saved many lives."

"How did you know to look for that airship?" Falkieth asked.

I shrugged. "Instinct, I guess. I didn't see any wagons on the ground, so I assumed that the cannon fire was coming from the sky."

Falkieth looked like she'd swallowed a lemon. "The old cannons were far too heavy to mount in an airship, so we never expected an attack from the sky," she said. "We'll have to start regular sky patrols above all the major cities. You there," she barked at two of the dragon riders. "Secure these cannons. We're bringing them back to Dragon's Table for further study."

"We don't have the manpower for regular sky patrols," the headmaster growled. "From the reports we've been getting, we're going to need everyone we can spare to fight in the coming conflict."

"Then we'll have to bring the older dragons out of retirement," Falkieth countered. "It isn't enough at this point to draw on the reserves. We have to protect our people, no matter what."

They finished examining the wreckage, then ordered me to take them to Ragor. When we arrived in the clearing, the dragon's wound had been treated and bandaged. Kade and the other riders were half-finished building a small shelter around him.

"We're not going to be able to move him for a few days," one of the riders explained, "so we'll have to keep him here until he's recovered."

We all pitched in to help, and then Lessie and I returned home while the other riders scoured the skies, searching for any other enemy airships that might be lurking. I held my breath the whole flight home, fearing we'd missed something and that Lessie and I might be shot out of the sky at any time.

"Don't be silly," Lessie chided as we touched down outside the stables. She turned her long, sinewy neck around so she could nuzzle me in the saddle. *"They didn't send more than one ship. This was a stealth mission to gauge our defenses."*

"I know," I said, nuzzling her back. Hopping down, I led Lessie into the stables to put away her tack and rub her down for the night.

We'd made it back safe, for now. Whether or not we'd continue to be safe depended entirely on whether the council took this threat seriously or decided to keep their heads buried in the sand and ignore just how hopelessly outgunned we were.

13

W hen I woke up the next morning, we were unofficially at war.

Dammit, I thought as I trudged into the mess hall, my limbs still heavy with exhaustion. I'd slept the entire morning away, which normally would have been fine since it was the weekend, but I'd been planning on going down to the shop to help Carina out and fill her in on everything. She probably heard the cannon fire last night and was out of her mind with worry. The morning was gone now, along with it the busiest time for us on Sundays, but maybe I could still go down and hang out with her for the afternoon.

"No can do," Rhia said as we ate lunch together. "There's a lockdown on campus right now. No one gets to come or go without permission from the headmaster himself."

"Of course there is," I groaned, not at all surprised. I'd have to send a letter to Carina, and she wouldn't be happy about that in the slightest. But after what happened last night, I couldn't blame the academy for being concerned.

Trying not to feel too trapped by the new restrictions, I went for a walk in the garden, trying to sort out my thoughts. I wished Jallis were here so I could talk to him. I wondered how he was doing at the camp. Had they put him on border patrol, so close to the Zallabarians and those nasty cannons? I shuddered at the thought of him and Kadryn being shot down by one, like poor Ragor and Ullion had been yesterday. I was so thankful that they'd merely been injured, and that they'd both make a full recovery. If they had been permanently crippled, or killed...

"Zara!" a fellow dragon rider cadet yelled as she rushed by. "The headmaster's summoned all rider cadets to the training room."

Tension dug into my shoulders as I jogged after her. The training room was a smaller, separate building from the academy, where cadets came for combat and physical fitness training. Major Falkieth and the headmaster both waited for us inside, and the other eight cadets were already lined up. I was pleased to see that Ullion was with us, looking relatively healthy —they must have gotten the same mage who healed me to treat him last night, for he didn't look like he was favoring his injured leg, or in pain at all. I gave him a quick smile as I lined up with the others.

"Cadets," the headmaster addressed us once we were all standing at attention. "Last night was a trying ordeal for all of us. For the first time in a century, a foreign power crossed into our territory and attacked our capital. If not for the actions of Miss Kenrook and Miss Thomas, we could have lost many lives last

---

night. We owe them a debt of gratitude for their quick thinking and decisive action."

The headmaster inclined his head toward us, and the other cadets burst into applause, whooping and cheering. But they quickly quieted when the headmaster and Major Falkieth stood in silence, and the mood grew somber again.

"While neither side has officially declared war, last night was the opening salvo, and the ten of you participated in your first battle. As of right now, you have all been put on active duty, and have the rank of Private, First Class."

No one said a word, but tension and excitement rippled through the ranks. I gritted my teeth. Of course they were going to put us on active duty rather than protect these cadets and their not-yet-grown dragons. I'd known that, and though in my heart I knew I'd do whatever it took to protect my friends and family, I hated that others were putting their lives on the line.

Lessie's consciousness rubbed up against my mind. *"You have to remember they signed up for this, Zara,"* she said. *"When they enrolled in the academy, when they went to the hatching ceremony and laid their hands upon those dragon eggs, they knew this day might come."*

"Despite these grim circumstances, there is some good news," the headmaster said, drawing my attention back to him. "Quoronis has decided to sit out the conflict, which means that we will only need to deal with Zallabar and Traggar, whose alliance still holds firm."

Yes! I crowed mentally, and I could feel Lessie's elation as well.

Lord Tavarian must have successfully convinced Quoronis to back down. Did that mean he was coming home soon? I could hardly wait to see him.

"However, Zallabar alone is a formidable opponent, especially after the demonstration last night, and there is no telling what might happen next," Falkieth butted in. "For all we know, the ship that attacked us last night was Traggaran, and they were using cannons given to them by Zallabar. I would not be surprised in the slightest if Traggar agreed to ally with them simply for a chance to get their hands on that technology."

Right. I'd never been to Traggar myself, but from what I understood, theirs was an isolationist, almost barbaric culture, and largely reliant on their navy. They were also hostile and bloodthirsty, more than happy to get their hands on any new weapons that would help them continue to conquer other countries.

"Clearly, we need more information, and that is where you will come in handy," the headmaster continued. "The ten of you will be departing for the border in stages—four of you will be sent to patrol the channel, and the other six will be patrolling the Zallabarian border. You will have two days to prepare and say goodbye to your loved ones."

Two days? I thought, alarmed. Would Tavarian be back in two days? And what did he think of this? Did he know that Lessie and I were being sent to the border, even though we weren't even close to finishing our training? I was almost sure he would object if he were here, since he was not fond of using dragons during wartime to begin with. But he wasn't here, and I would be forced to comply.

Major Falkieth, sensing the unease rippling through the line, addressed us again. "Don't look so grim, riders," she said, her normally rough voice softening a bit with encouragement. "This is a fairly safe mission, or at least as safe as anything can be in wartime. Heroics are not only *not* required of you, they are actively discouraged. Your duty will be to observe any incursions of airships or troop movements and report them to the regional headquarters where you have been assigned. They will send out regular forces to deal with the enemy. Your smaller dragons are ideal for the task, since you will be able to hide more easily in the clouds, and you will help save countless lives."

The cadets seemed to relax a little at this, and I could feel Lessie's excitement through the bond. *"Finally, a chance to be useful!"* she exclaimed. *"We are going to be good at this, Zara."*

"I know we will," I said, smiling inwardly at her. I loved that she always seemed to find the silver lining, the positive outlook, no matter how dire the situation. And in truth, I was happy we were given a task that would keep us out of harm's way while still allowing us to help with the war effort. We could survive for a week or two, until Lord Tavarian returned. I was certain he'd call us back once he realized what was going on.

The headmaster dismissed the rest of the cadets but ordered me to stay behind. "I wanted to let you know I received word from Lord Tavarian," he said. "He should be returning to Dragon's Table in a week's time to report to the council."

"Good." I figured he would be, but hearing it out loud still filled me with relief. "Is there any way that I can wait until he comes back? I'd like to speak to him in person before I go."

Major Falkieth shook her head. "Unless you can give a compelling reason as to why you have to stay back, there's nothing we can do. The general will be very unhappy if you don't arrive with the others, especially since you have firsthand experience with the guns."

"That's why we're sending you out there," the headmaster admitted, looking rather guilty. "Normally we would have had you and Miss Thomas stay behind, but you are the only two riders who've dealt with these cannons up close and personal, so you are needed. Miss Thomas will be going to the Zallabarian border, and you'll be headed to the channel."

"We're being separated?" I asked, my stomach plummeting. "We can't both go to the border?"

"I'm sorry," the headmaster said. "But that's where you're needed."

I clenched my jaw, my insides a mess of roiling emotions. First Tavarian, then Jallis, and now Rhia. My friends were being stripped from me, one by one. But there was nothing I could say, so I forced my protests back and beat a retreat to the stables so I could cuddle with Lessie for a bit and feel sorry for myself.

Every girl needs a good sulk now and again.

"I'm not even going to be able to see Jallis," I grumbled to her as I leaned against her side, the two of us curled up in the hay together. *"He's in a camp by the border, not at the channel."* I hadn't heard from him at all since he'd left, and by the time he got around to sending me a letter, I'd be long gone. *"I'll be surrounded by strangers."*

"*You'll have me,*" Lessie reminded me, nudging me with her snout. "*Besides, it's not as if you don't know how to make friends. You didn't know anyone when you came to Dragon's Table, either.*"

"Yeah, but we're going to a military camp," I said. "We're going to be with a bunch of stuffy riders and stubborn soldiers who think they're invincible. That general may have asked for me, but that doesn't mean the others are going to take me seriously. Most of them will probably think I'm just some stupid ground-dweller."

"*Not when they see you riding in on* my *back,*" Lessie growled. She lifted her head so she could toss it. "*It will be impossible for them to look upon me without basking in my magnificence.*"

I snorted with laughter, and she grinned, flashing her dragon teeth at me. "*I knew that would make you laugh,*" she said, nuzzling me. "*Cheer up, Zara. At least we'll be flying together, and the more time we spend in the air, the harder it will be for Salcombe to get us if he ever gets free of the Zallabarians. And even if he does come to find us, we'll be surrounded by soldiers most of the time.*"

"*True,*" I said, though I was dubious. While Salcombe wasn't stupid enough to attack a military camp, he was desperate and very clever— a *dangerous* combination. If anyone could figure out how to snatch me out from under the army's nose, it would be Salcombe. I'd have to let them know that he was still hunting me so proper precautions could be taken.

"*They must really want me,*" I said to Lessie as I stretched my legs out in the sand, "*because as far as I can tell, you and I are two walking, talking liabilities.*"

14

O n the eve of our departure, I reported to the meeting room with Kade, Ullion, and a girl called Daria to be briefed on our destination. Headmaster Caparro and Major Falkieth were there, but the briefing was led by a new face— Lieutenant Bellmont, an officer from the war department.

"While Zallabar has still not declared open war despite that underhanded attack on our capital," Bellmont was saying, "all indications are that Traggar's alliance with them still holds, and they will be joining in the impending war." He gestured to a map on the wall, pointing to a cluster of islands north of Elantia. "Traggar is made up of these six main islands here, plus the dozens of smaller islands that run all the way up the coast here." He traced a path farther north with his white-gloved finger, then brought it back down to the stretch of ocean separating the islands from the mainland. "You will be monitoring the channel, here, for any signs of unusual activity."

Bellmont then took a few minutes to describe the terrain, and I did my best not to tune him out. I'd already spent the last two days refreshing my knowledge of Traggar. The channel was of variable width and took three to five hours to cross, depending on which point you started at from the mainland or which island you were trying to get to. It was extremely dangerous to attempt the crossing during storms due to the rocks and cliffs, and dragons could be battered badly by the treacherous winds or even struck by lightning.

Unfortunately, the northern border near the channel was never considered a likely front in the last century. Elantia had only ever had a few skirmishes with them, when Traggar attempted to grab pieces of the continent and were driven back. As a result of being out of touch with them for decades, we were not well-prepared as a country to deal with them. I only knew a few phrases of Traggaran since I'd never traveled there. The country's perpetual rainy season and boggy lands didn't make it an ideal vacation destination, and it wasn't a promising location for digging up relics, either.

"Traggar is currently ruled by Zolar the Third," the lieutenant said, tapping at a sketch posted to the wall. The man in question looked like a thug, with beady eyes, close-cropped hair, and a harsh, forbidding face. "Like the rest of his people, he is not at all friendly to Elantians, and should you be captured, he will have your dragons tortured until you give up every bit of intel you have. Traggarans are also extremely untrustworthy, and any contract or promise he might offer you will not be honored. I would highly advise doing anything possible to avoid capture should you run across them for any reason."

The four of us shuddered. I wasn't surprised to hear this about the Traggarans—from what I understood, King Zolar was a despot who had a penchant for divorcing and exiling his wives when he tired of them, and he didn't trust foreigners. Of course, he wasn't the kind of man who kept his promises or was interested in making peace with other nations.

"Since your primary objective is reconnaissance, it is doubtful that you will have to deal with the Traggarans directly," Lieutenant Bellmont said, as if to placate us. He then continued to give us the highlights on Traggar, and the more I heard, the less I liked. Apparently, Traggar was heavily involved in the slave trade —since they'd concentrated on shipbuilding, they had a strong navy, which they'd used to conquer various islands and areas in the southern climates that they cruelly exploited for natural resources. While slave trading was illegal in Traggar itself, it was *not* illegal in the southern islands, and thus it had become a booming industry for them.

"I don't think I'd feel guilty at all if we ended up having to kill some of them," Lessie informed me in a haughty tone.

I hid my smile. *"Neither do I. Although Lieutenant Bellmont's briefing seems a bit biased. After all, a population of over three million has to have a few good eggs, don't you think?"*

"I don't care about good eggs," Lessie informed me, and I could just see her tossing her head in my mind's eye. *"I just care about keeping you safe."*

"Something funny, Private Kenrook?"

The lieutenant's sharp voice brought me back to the present, and I blinked. "No, sir," I said. I guess I hadn't managed to hide my smile after all.

The lieutenant held my gaze for a long moment. "While scouting and defense will be your priority, you should all make an effort to learn the language and history in your spare time," he finally said, his gaze sweeping away from me to take in the others. "Learning as much as you can about the enemy is crucial to winning, no matter how small or large your part in the war is."

With that, he dismissed us.

The four of us went to our respective rooms to finish packing. In just a few hours, we'd be heading out, and who knew when we'd be coming back to the academy? Hell, would we come back at all? I knew from studying military history that wars often went on for years. Being out there, living and working on a military base, would teach us far more than we could ever learn at the academy. There might not be anything left for the professors to teach us.

It was a sobering thought, and one that made my stomach twist with dread. In my heart, I was still a reluctant cadet. I was still coming to terms with the fact that I was now officially conscripted.

I pressed my new uniform, checked and rechecked my bags, then tucked Lessie in. I would have stayed with her in the stables all night, but the stable master kicked me out, and I trudged back to my room, miserable. Changing into my pajamas, I slid beneath the sheets and closed my eyes, trying to sleep. But all I could see was Ragor's ruined wing, the sound of cannon fire echoing in my ears. And we were only going to see more of that...

A knock on my door pulled me from my grim thoughts, and I jumped out of bed, my blood pumping. "Yes?" I cried, peering through the peephole. I wasn't stupid enough to throw the door open, not after Salcombe had successfully kidnapped me once from campus. It took a minute for my eyes to adjust, but soon, Mrs. Browning, the residence hall mistress, came into view and I opened the door.

"Sorry to wake you, Miss Kenrook," she said, "but you have a visitor."

"A visitor?" I frowned. "Who?"

"Lord Tavarian." She gave a slight smile at my stunned look. "Normally I would not allow visitors past curfew, but in this case, I will make an exception. He is waiting for you in the lounge."

"I'll be right there," I blurted, then slammed the door in her face. I shucked off my pajamas and hurriedly threw on my clothes, then checked my wild hair in the mirror and smoothed it down a bit. Not that I was trying to impress him, but I did have *some* dignity.

"Miss Kenrook." Lord Tavarian rose from his chair by the fire as I entered the room. He looked well put together, as always, in one of those dark suits he always wore, his long, black hair pulled neatly back at the nape of his neck. But there were shadows beneath his eyes, tension in his angular face that spoke of exhaustion. And something flickered in his silver eyes, an odd look I couldn't quite place my finger on...

"Lord Tavarian." I crossed the room in quick strides, then stopped short just before him. That familiar tension hummed in the air between us, and I paused, unsure how to greet him. "How did you get back here so fast?" I asked, trying to cover up my awkwardness.

"I had a bit of help from Muza." A brief smile flickered across his features, but it died as those silver eyes flicked up and down my body, taking me in. "You are unharmed? I heard about what happened with Salcombe."

I sucked in a breath as I recognized the odd look in his eyes as guilt. "He didn't hurt me. Just threatened me."

His mouth tightened in a grim line. "I dropped by the estate to check on you on my way back to Dragon's Table, and was horrified to find you and Lessie gone. If Mr. and Mrs. Barton hadn't received a letter from the headmaster explaining where you were and what had happened, I would have torn apart the countryside looking for you."

His heated words made my skin prickle with warmth. Salcombe would have never said something like that to me. Even when we'd been on good terms, he'd always kept me at arm's distance —ours was a relationship of mutual convenience, not affection. When I'd first met Tavarian, I'd painted him with the same cold, calculated strokes that Salcombe presented to the world.

But I was wrong. He wasn't cold, just armored. He kept his heart protected to shelter the many secrets he held close to his chest.

"I'm so glad you made it back," I said, with feeling. "You were gone for so long that I was worried you'd offended the Quoronians and they'd decided to take you prisoner."

Tavarian chuckled darkly. "The Quoronians would have sent me back in a box, in pieces, if that had been the case."

"Not helping." I scowled.

He sighed. "I'm sorry I left you," he said, looking chagrined. "I wish I never had. If your friends hadn't been there to rescue you..."

"Please, don't." I held up my hand before he could continue beating himself up. "You couldn't have known that Salcombe had a tracking spell on me. If it were anyone else who'd been looking for me, I'd probably still be tucked away in that little valley, safe and sound."

His eyes flared. "Location spell? The headmaster didn't mention that." Gesturing to the chairs, he made me sit down, then fill him in on everything.

By the time I was done, Tavarian's face was set in a deep scowl. "Of course he would use your hair for the tracking spell," he said, raking his eyes over my fiery mane. "You have so much of it that you wouldn't notice if a few strands got clipped here or there." He paused. "If shaving your head would cancel out the spell, I would do it in a heartbeat."

My hands flew to my scalp. "That's not funny," I growled.

"Actually, it is a little funny," he said, surprising me as the corner of his mouth quirked up. But that brief hint of levity disappeared, replaced by something that looked very much like pride. "You've come a long way, Miss Kenrook. Escaping Salcombe's clutches, downing that airship, and now you're headed out on your first mission. I'm impressed."

I cleared my throat around the lump that was trying to form there. "Yeah," I said quietly. "And all because you took a chance on a street rat."

"You've never been a street rat." His eyes sharpened, and he pulled my dragon blade from a leather pouch sitting by the chair. My heart leaped as he handed it to me, along with my lock pick and goggles. "This blade is proof of that, and one day, when this is all over, we will trace your lineage and find out who your parents were. You deserve to know to which house you belong."

"Thanks." I smiled, meeting his gaze. "But I already know which house I belong to."

There was a flicker of surprise, followed by sudden warmth, as he smiled at me. "Careful," he said. "If you keep talking like that, I'll start to believe you actually enjoy being a dragon rider."

I raised my eyebrows. "I do enjoy being a dragon rider. I just don't enjoy the part where I have to place my dragon's life in danger just because my country couldn't get its shit together."

Tavarian sighed. "If I could, I'd send you straight back to the valley," he said. "But I can't countermand the general's orders. I sent him a letter regarding Salcombe, and the danger he poses not just to you, but to Elantia and the world as a whole, but I will not hold my breath. The military will merely see this as the ravings of a madman over magical 'mumbo jumbo' and will not take it seriously."

"Great." I pinched the bridge of my nose, trying to relieve the pressure of an oncoming headache. "Speaking of Salcombe, I ran into some of his friends a few weeks ago."

"Oh?" Tavarian's eyes sharpened. "What did you discover?"

I filled him in on my trip to the catacombs, what I'd witnessed and overheard in that sepulcher. "It sounds like Red Beard, whoever he is, knows where the piece of heart is."

Tavarian sighed. "If you'd been able to get a better description of him, I'd be able to notify the city guards to keep a look out for him," he said. "I'll send word to have those catacombs scoured and the temple searched. Perhaps one of the temple staff will be able to tell us something useful, or some of the acolytes are still lurking there."

"Maybe." I doubted any of Salcombe's followers would continue to meet in the catacombs, not after I'd spooked them. They would have found a new hiding place.

"I do admit that I assumed Salcombe would be traveling with the piece of heart on him, since he needs it to keep up his health," Tavarian said, shifting the subject back to the heart. "But I suppose it makes sense that he would have found an alternative. Better to keep an object like that hidden rather than take it place to place while you're on the run. I checked my dispatches when I stopped at the estate, and read the reports about Salcombe's detention in Zallabar. His estate here in Zuar City is under guard, and if he manages to escape the

Zallabarian authorities and return here, he will be apprehended."

"Isn't there any way that we can snatch him away from them?" I asked. "Since he's Elantian?"

"Perhaps we would have had a chance six months ago, but not now," Tavarian said heavily. "Besides, there is no time for me to attempt it just now. I am leaving for Traggar to see if I can convince them to stand down as well."

My eyes widened. "You can't be serious. They'll eat you alive!" Hadn't Lieutenant Bellmont just finished telling me how much the Traggarans hated us?

I waited for Tavarian to tell me that I was being dramatic, that everything would be fine. But his face settled into grim lines that made my stomach twist.

"It's true that my chances of success are not very good," he said, and for the first time since I'd met him, I hated that he was agreeing with me. "But the Traggarans will hear me out none-theless. King Zolar is highly capricious, and it is quite possible that he may turn against Zallabar if they annoy him enough. With the right words, I might be able to facilitate such a change of heart."

"Right." The Traggarans weren't known for keeping their promises, and that included their alliance with Zallabar. If a better opportunity came knocking...

"If I succeed, and Traggar backs down, your presence will no longer be needed at the channel," Tavarian went on, rising from his chair. I stood as well, my eyelids heavy. I needed to catch a few hours of sleep so I didn't fall out of the saddle tomorrow. "The general would be much more amenable to giving you an extended leave so I can spend more time training you and Lessie."

The impact of his words hit me, and I blinked away the sudden tears. "Really? You can do that?" I'd thought Lessie and I would be stuck for years, but if this was true...we might be able to come home in a matter of weeks.

He smiled. "I do have *some* influence around here." But his amusement faded, and he took my hand. "I have every intention of making it back alive from Traggar, but there is a very good chance I might not. If things should go wrong, I have made provisions for you and Lessie in my will."

I stared at him. "Your will?"

"Of course. You are both members of my house. No matter what happens, you will always be taken care of."

Tears sprang to my eyes, a well of emotions rising inside me. Overwhelmed, I threw my arms around his neck in a spontaneous hug that surprised us both. Tavarian had already done so much for me, but this...

"Thank you," I murmured, pressing a kiss to his cheek. A shockwave rippled through me at the gesture, and I felt it hit him too. What was wrong with me?

Tavarian, who had initially frozen, suddenly wrapped his arms around me, returning the hug. "Stay safe," he said roughly, his cheek warm against mine.

Embarrassed, I stepped out of his arms and hastily beat a retreat to my room. But as I put distance between us, I recalled the way his body had stiffened just a brief moment before he'd wrapped those strong arms around my body and sank against me. As if affection was a foreign concept to him.

When was the last time Tavarian had been hugged?

15

After a quick but emotional farewell with Rhia, Lessie and I took off early the next morning with Kade, Ullion, and Daria. My stomach fluttered with nervous excitement as we flew —I'd never visited a military camp and had little idea of what to expect. Would we be living in tents? Mrs. Browning had made us pack bedrolls, mess kits, and other items suitable for camping. While I was an expert at camping thanks to years of traveling through forests and jungles, searching for buried ruins, I wasn't looking forward to camping year-round. Summer only lasted a few short months, and then the harsh winter winds would be bearing down upon us. I was *not* looking forward to camping in a tent with snowdrifts piling up around me.

"If Tavarian's mission to Traggar goes well, we might not be stuck at the camp through winter," Lessie reminded me as we soared over rolling hills dotted with greenery. *"We'll be back at the hidden valley in no time, training with Muza again."*

I could tell that the prospect of seeing Tavarian's dragon again cheered Lessie very much, so I patted her neck and smiled. *"I hope he comes through, then,"* I said, ignoring the feeling of dread in my stomach. Tavarian must be good at his job, but I'd never seen him in action as a diplomat, and everything I'd read and heard about the Traggarans told me that they would not be easy to negotiate with. Their hatred for Elantians might be stronger than their capricious tendencies, and if that was the case, no amount of pleading or bribing would sway them from their path.

It took us twelve hours to fly to the northern border, with several stops along the way to allow the dragons to rest and for us to relieve ourselves. They did not hunt, since more food would only slow us down, and though the riders had packed dried meat and hard biscuits for the journey, we were all ravenous by the time we landed.

As instructed by Lieutenant Bellmont, the four of us touched down in a wide clearing next to the dragon stables. I was pleased to see the camp was not made up of tents, but buildings constructed of solid timber. The stables were the largest building, with enough room to comfortably house twenty dragons, and I imagined the other large building, located toward the center of camp, were the barracks we'd be staying in.

Several officers strode out from one of the smaller buildings as we dismounted, their expressions stern. As they approached, close enough to look us all over, I was able to read the surprise and derision all over their faces. They were not pleased to see us, I realized with dismay.

"Greetings," a tow-headed woman with close-cropped hair said stiffly. Her grey eyes swept over us as we fell in line, and I had to fight against a scowl at the dismissive look she gave us. "My name is Colonel Roche, and I am in command." She gestured to one of the officers, who pulled a pen and notepad from his breast pocket, then stepped up to Kade, who stood at the front of the line. "Name and rank."

Kade gave it to her, and she went through the rest of us quickly. "Zara Kenrook," I said when she got to me, third in line.

Her grey eyes narrowed. "The ground-dweller," she said. "Yes, we've all heard of the troublemaker that Lord Tavarian took in." She glanced over my shoulder at my dragon, as if she couldn't believe Lessie had actually chosen me. "General Sarte requested you because of your 'experience' with the enemy's cannons." The skepticism in her voice made me want to shove her head into one of those cannons so she could get her own personal "experience."

Too bad we didn't have any cannons around here.

"Regardless of whatever friends you may have in high places," the colonel went on, "you'll be expected to follow the rules just like everyone else. Thieving and insubordination will not be tolerated at this camp. Is that understood?"

She shoved her nose into my face, eyes glittering with disgust. I swallowed back my rage and forced myself to nod. "Yes, ma'am."

"I can't hear you!"

"YES, MA'AM!" I shouted, loud enough to blow her eardrums off.

She nodded coldly as she stepped back, unfazed by my sudden volume. "Good. Now get your dragons settled in, and report to the quartermaster."

The four of us turned and led our dragons to the stables. The stable master gave our dragons a critical once-over as they were introduced to him, then shook his head. "Babies," he muttered in disappointment. "They sent us babies."

Lessie dropped her head so it was level with his and let out a low growl. But that only made the stable master scowl at me. "Get your dragon under control," he snapped at me, "or I'll ground you both for a week."

Gee, I'm sure that'll help with the war effort, I thought sarcastically, but I put a hand on Lessie's flank, warning her silently. Disgruntled, she backed off, though she continued to glare at the man.

The stable master finished his inspection of our dragons, then assigned stalls to each of them. "Dinner will be served at the mess hall in forty minutes," he said as he walked away. "I'd get a move on if I were you."

Gritting my teeth, I removed Lessie's tack and hung it up, then grabbed the brushes and tools hanging from the walls and gave her a quick grooming. As I ran a hand over her scales, checking for rot or damage, another dragon poked his large head through the door.

"Kadryn!" I exclaimed, my lousy mood falling away instantly. Lessie jumped to her feet with a squeak of excitement so she could rub her snout against his.

"Jallis must be here, then!" Lessie said, and I could hear the grin in her mental voice. *"Are you excited to see him?"*

"It'll be nice to see a friendly face," I said, smiling. *"Especially who doesn't think we're a bunch of useless kids."*

"We'll show them," Lessie said in a heated voice as she settled back down onto her bed of hay so I could finish grooming her. *"Those soldiers are just jealous."*

I smiled at her haughty confidence, but inside I was worried. As much as I hated to admit it, Colonel Roche was right to be concerned about us. Lessie and I weren't thieves—or at least I wasn't, not anymore—but we weren't exactly the best at following rules. The military virtues of discipline and obedience, especially *blind* obedience, would not come easily to either one of us. If we weren't careful, we could find ourselves grounded.

Being grounded would be safer than patrolling the border, I tried to tell myself, but my heart wasn't in it. Yes, I wanted Lessie and me to be safe, but we weren't the type to sit back and do nothing. If there was something we could do to help, we wanted to be a part of it.

I finished Lessie's grooming just in time for her dinner to arrive —two whole sheep, freshly slaughtered. Her hunger instantly reminded me of my own, and I left her to enjoy her meal so I could find my own food.

After a short visit with the quartermaster, who assigned me a bottom bunk in the women's section of the barracks, we made our way to the mess hall. Joining the line, I grabbed a tray and scanned the room, searching for Jallis. It didn't take long to find him—he was at one of the long tables on the far side of the room, talking and laughing with a group of men and women. I frowned, noting that they all appeared to be officers, including Jallis. Was that a lieutenant pin on his breast?

After grabbing my food—a simple meal of stewed meat, beans, and brown rice—I made my way over to the table. Jallis glanced my way as I approached, and his face slackened with shock.

"Zara?" He shot to his feet instantly, his fork clattering against his tray. "What are you doing here?"

"I've been stationed here, same as you, apparently." I frowned, noting the complete lack of warmth in his eyes. He seemed... dismayed to find me here, and my jaw tightened reflexively in anger. "Is that going to be a problem?"

"No, of course not," he said hurriedly. "It's just that I didn't think you and Lessie would be called out so soon. I thought they'd give you more time to train."

"They asked for us because we have experience with the cannons," I said, raising an eyebrow. "Mind introducing me to your friends?"

"Oh. Yes, of course." Jallis seemed flustered. He introduced me to the three other officers seated with him, who all turned out to be dragon riders as well. "This is Manfried," he said, indicating the stocky, silver-haired man next to him. "He and I are partners."

"Nice to meet you," I said.

He grunted. "I thought Lyton here was a whippersnapper when

they first assigned him to me, but you seem even less experienced." He pinned his sharp gaze on me. "Have you seen battle?"

"As a matter of fact, I have," I said, lifting my chin. "An airship attacked Zuar City a couple of nights ago. They had two of those new cannons mounted on the ship, and they tried to shoot us out of the sky during a training exercise in Briarwood Forest." Mouths dropped open in shock, and I had to hide a smirk. "One rider and his dragon were badly wounded, but luckily no one else was hurt because my friend Rhia and I flew up into the clouds and destroyed the airship. If we hadn't used dragon fire to destroy that airship, it might have injured or killed many more dragons. Those shrapnel cannons are deadly."

The officers said nothing, and after a second, I realized silence had fallen over the entire mess hall. "Well, that's what we've been up to," I said brightly. "What about you?"

Jallis gave me a lopsided smile, quickly recovering from his shock. "Let's catch up a bit later," he offered, ignoring the disapproving frown on his partner's face. "We can compare notes when I go tuck in Kadryn for the night."

"Tuck in," Manfried snorted. "It's a dragon, not a baby."

Jallis's cheeks pinkened, but he merely said, "It's an important part of our bonding ritual. You know that."

Recognizing I was dismissed, I trudged over to the table where Kade and the others were sitting. "I should have warned you," Kade said apologetically as I sat down. "The officers aren't allowed to fraternize with us."

"I didn't realize that Jallis would become a lieutenant so quickly," I muttered.

"He and his dragon are older, with more experience, and he comes from a prestigious family," Ullion explained. "More than likely, his father purchased the commission for him."

"Of course he did." I sighed, trying to extinguish the spark of jealousy. What did I care if Jallis was an officer and I wasn't? Officers had to deal with more responsibility, which was exactly what I didn't want.

"I guess this means none of us are getting partnered up together," I said, glancing over to Jallis and the older rider he'd been paired with.

Daria shook her head. "They'll want to send us out with someone more experienced," she said. "To make sure we're safe."

Meaning someone who's rigid and unwilling to think outside the box, I grumbled quietly to myself as I ate my food. What Rhia and I did, flying up into the clouds and taking out that airship on our own initiative, was exactly the kind of forward thinking the military disapproved of. Dammit, I missed her already. I understood why she and I had been split up, but I still hated it.

Observe and report, I reminded myself. As long as I stuck to the parameters of the mission, I shouldn't need to break the rules, right?

After dinner, I went back to the stables, hoping to see Jallis again. Sure enough, he was in Kadryn's stall, gently petting the larger dragon's head as he sat in the hay with him. The stiff, formal officer was gone, replaced with the kind, caring young man with a gift for comforting animals.

"Hey." I leaned over the stall gate and smiled at him.

"Hey." He twisted around to look at me, a rueful smile on his face. "Fancy seeing you here."

I opened the gate and let myself in. "You really *aren't* happy to see me," I said, making a face as I sat down and leaned my back against the opposite wall.

Jallis sighed. "I'm just surprised Lord Tavarian allowed it," he said. "Does he know you're here?"

I nodded. "I spoke to him the night before we left. He wasn't happy about it, but General Sarte was insistent that Rhia and I be deployed since we're the only two who have experience dealing with the cannons. I'm not sure why that's necessary since we're just going to be doing reconnaissance missions, but it's not like I can ask." I shrugged.

"Rhia?" Jallis frowned. "Is she here too?"

I shook my head. "She was sent to the Zallabarian border."

"I see."

The two of us fell silent, Jallis turning his attention back to petting his dragon. I was about to leave so I could spend time with my own dragon when Jallis shifted, reaching for a leather pouch sitting in the hay.

"I brought this for you," he said, handing it to me. "Wax and star blossom oil," he added as I pulled out two containers. "You'll want to treat your gear with this before you go out on patrol. It helps keep them waterproof."

"Thanks," I said, a little surprised. "Is the weather nasty out there?"

Jallis grimaced. "Even on good days we end up getting hit by rain and squalls."

"Ugh." I was not looking forward to that. "Have you seen any hostilities yet?"

"No, but the Traggarans are assembling a large navy in one of the southern ports that might be intended to cross and invade Elantia. Manfried and I regularly pass by there to check on it, and this armada is growing by the day. They're even loading the ships up with large amounts of supplies."

"Then they're definitely going to be used soon," I said. Biting my lower lip, I considered the problem. "Is there a way to burn the ships before they can launch their armada? Maybe we can swoop down there with our dragons and light them all up."

"Not without putting them at great risk," Jallis said. "We'd have to get close enough for the fire to reach the ships, and the port is heavily fortified with those heavy, old-style cannons. We'd be blown out of the sky. Not to mention we're not allowed to make a move," he added. "We're not officially at war, after all."

"Right." I fought the urge to roll my eyes. The Zallabarians had already attacked us, and yet we couldn't retaliate. I understood why we had to wait—we didn't want to strike before Tavarian had a chance to convince the Traggarans to stand down—but it was still frustrating to have to sit on our hands and do nothing.

"Well, I better turn in for the night. I've got to be up early for a meeting." Jallis rose, dusting the hay off his uniform. He extended a hand to help me to my feet, and I took it. The familiar current of warmth passed between us, but instead of pulling me against him, as he would have in the past, Jallis merely smiled. "Good night."

"Good night," I echoed. Patting Kadryn on the head, I followed Jallis out of the stall, then went to join Lessie.

"At least it sounds like Traggar hasn't gotten its hands on the new cannons," I told her as I settled in next to her for a snuggle. I wasn't sure if it was "proper" for riders to snuggle with their dragons when on active duty, but frankly I didn't care. *"Maybe that means their alliance with Zallabar isn't as solid as we've been led to believe."*

"Very possible," Lessie agreed. *"As far as blowing up that armada, I think we could do it on a foggy night, when the Traggarans are unable to see well enough to use their cannons effectively. We do not need the same level of visibility to set the ships on fire—we merely need to get close enough and aim in the general direction."*

"That's an idea," I said, though I wasn't as confident about it as Lessie. After all, the dragons could easily get hurt by crashing into buildings or impaling their fragile wings on masts.

"You should talk to the colonel about it," Lessie said eagerly. *"The sooner we can get the others on board, the sooner we can try it out."*

"*Whoa, there.*" I stroked Lessie's side, a little alarmed at her enthusiasm. "*We're not officially at war yet, remember? Besides, the colonel will dismiss the plan as reckless and foolhardy. We'll just have to wait for a good opportunity to make a difference.*"

Lessie grumbled at that, but she didn't argue. We cuddled for a little longer before I turned in for the night, trudging back to the barracks so I could lay my bedroll out on the hard bunk. A few soldiers were already tucked in, snoring away, and I gritted my teeth, wishing I'd thought to bring earplugs.

Better get used to it, Zara, I told myself as I tried to tune it out. I valued my privacy more than almost anything else, but I realized as another soldier moved about the space, stark naked, that privacy was quickly becoming a thing of the past.

This is going to be a loooooong night.

16

Despite my misgivings about the military, fitting in at camp was surprisingly easy. In many ways, it was not unlike the academy, with its rules and rigid schedule. We all ate together, bathed together, worked together, drilled together, and slept together.

Many of us literally.

On my way to the mess hall, I rolled my eyes as moans came from a closet. I wouldn't be even remotely surprised if I opened the door and found Kade—he was a bit of a cocky bastard, and had no problem getting women into his bed despite being one of the youngest men on the base.

If I was honest with myself, I was a bit jealous that *I* wasn't the one in there, with my legs wrapped around Jallis. But we were on different shifts, and almost never saw each other. The night I'd arrived had been his day off—he and Kadryn were assigned to night shift, while Lessie and I were on day. And the few times

I happened to be in the mess hall with him, he kept his distance, not wanting to make a misstep in front of his fellow officers.

Man, I need to get laid, I thought grumpily as I shoveled porridge in my mouth. I wouldn't be so grumpy about his continued cold shoulder if not for the fact that I hadn't been intimate with anyone in the last six months. But it wasn't as if there were any good prospects here. A few men had made lewd advances on me, but they were practically thugs, not appealing in the slightest. And most of the older riders kept their distance from me, disapproving of the way I'd come into my birthright, much like Jallis's mother, Lady Lyton, had been. I wondered if Jallis even attempted to change their minds about me, or if he kept his head down and allowed them to think as they would.

Finished with breakfast, I went out to the stables and saddled up Lessie for our shift. As I led her out into the blessedly sunny day, I saw Captain Gabin Fosse, my partner, waiting with his olive-green dragon, Mirn.

"Ready?" His eyes flicked over Lessie, who was half the size of his dragon. Fosse was in his late thirties, with sandy brown hair and a medium build, and handsome, if a bit boring, features. We'd been flying together for three days now, and while he wasn't particularly friendly, we were growing a bit more comfortable with each other.

"Yes, sir," I said as I swung myself up into the saddle. As captain, he outranked me by a mile. Gripping the reins, I waited until Mirn took off, his great wings kicking up dust in my face, before urging Lessie into the sky.

Though we had earpieces similar to the ones Tavarian had used while training Lessie and me, Fosse and I didn't speak much. I knew it wasn't because he was a man of few words; I'd seen him talking animatedly with the other officers at dinner. But I refused to let his dislike bother me, not when Lessie and I were doing what we loved most—flying. True, the wind was freezing, but I dressed warmly to compensate, and the shining sun, which rarely made an appearance out here, made things more bearable as it glittered off the waves below.

"It's beautiful," Lessie said happily as we soared along the coast, watching the gilded waves lap against the shore. From this height, far above the gulls and other marine birds, we could see the entire channel and all the ships on this particular stretch of coast, as well as the Traggaran islands floating off in the distance. It was the perfect place to keep track of our enemy.

Speaking of Traggar...I narrowed my eyes as I spotted a ship sailing across the channel toward the delta of the river Traice, which led directly to Puilin, Traggar's capital city. Lifting my hand to my face, I twisted the dial on the goggles Carina had given me and zoomed in to see if I could identify the ship. I had the night-vision goggles, too, but since we patrolled by day, I used my own even though they weren't regulation.

No markings, I thought as I studied the flag. Was it a ship from Elantia, or Zallabar? Could Tavarian be on it, headed for the capital to speak to the king? I knew he wouldn't be able to hitch a ride on Muza, not if he wanted to keep the dragon's existence a secret.

"I can't imagine how hard it must be, doing a job as difficult as Tavari-

an's without having his dragon by his side," I said to Lessie. *"I come to you for comfort all the time when things get rough, but he can't do that with Muza."*

Lessie didn't make a sound, but I felt her agreement and sympathy in the bond. *"Muza told me he feels guilty sometimes that he and Tavarian are forced to live separately. But Tavarian won't hear of it when Muza offers to come home. He wants his dragon to be free."*

I frowned. *"But is Muza really free?"* I asked. *"As long as the two of them are bound together, they still feel pain when they are separated. How is that freedom, when neither of them can move on from the other?"* I understood Tavarian's desire to keep Muza safe, but it seemed like the two of them were punishing themselves for no reason.

"Even if Tavarian did decide to bring Muza out of retirement, it would only bring trouble," Lessie said. *"Tavarian would have to admit to the council that he'd lied, and there would be consequences for that. He might lose his position, and what good would that do?"*

I exhaled. It was a tough situation. And yet I felt that there was still something more to this that had to do with the secret Lessie refused to divulge to me. If only I could ask Tavarian about it—

"Zara." Lessie's urgent voice pulled me away from my speculation. *"Down there. An Elantian ship."*

Craning my neck, I saw that there was, in fact, a vessel flying Elantian colors—red and gold. It was drifting there, without sails, rather low in the water.

"Fosse," I spoke into the device, waving a hand to get his attention. "There's an Elantian ship stranded in the channel. It looks like it's sinking."

Fosse looked toward where I pointed. "We are not a rescue team," he said. "Our job is to observe and report."

"Oh, come on," I say, a little exasperated. "Don't you think we should at least ask what happened? We're supposed to be gathering intel. What if they were attacked?"

Fosse was silent for a long moment. "Mirn is too large to be able to land on the ship's deck," he finally said. "We will circle above while you go down to check it out."

"Thank you, sir." I leaned into Lessie, gripping the pommel, and she immediately tucked her wings in and dove.

"Remember, it might be a false flag!" Fosse shouted into my earpiece, but I paid him no mind. Neither Lessie nor I spotted any weapons or other signs of danger on the ship, and between my goggles and her sharp vision, we should have. In fact, we didn't see anyone on board at all, which made me wonder if the ship was abandoned.

Snapping out her wings, Lessie glided onto the deserted deck. The ship immediately began to sink farther into the water, and we froze. Was it going to go under completely?

"It's fine," Lessie said after a few moments. The ship did sink a few feet, but now that we weren't moving, it stabilized. *"I'll wait here and warn you if the ship sinks more, or if I spot anything. Go below and see if you can find anyone."*

"I'm on it," I said, hopping off her back. My boots made no noise

as I hit the deck—I'd managed to convince the sergeant to let me keep them even though they weren't regulation. Cautiously, I climbed down the steps into the dim interior of the ship, my ears straining to pick up any sound. Faint groans drew me farther into the belly of the ship, and I struck a match from the book in my pocket, then used it to light a lamp sitting abandoned on a table.

The sounds were coming from the hold, toward the hull of the ship. The door was locked, but thankfully I had my magic lock pick with me, and in seconds, I was yanking it open.

"Dragon's balls," I swore as I waded in. Water sloshed around my boots as I made my way to the far corner of the hold, where the crew was trussed up, gagged, and half-buried by sacks of wheat. Pushing one of the sodden sacks aside, I reached for the nearest man and yanked his gag out.

"Thank Dariann," the man cried in Elantian, invoking the name of the deity that we used to worship centuries ago. I relaxed, recognizing them as my own countrymen. Drawing my knife, I cut him free, then ordered him to move the sacks of wheat aside so I could free the others—seven men in total, of varying ages, and two boys that couldn't be more than fourteen years of age. They all thanked me fervently as they raced past me to escape the bowels of the ship. Not that I could blame them—judging by the slowly rising water level, they must have been terrified that they were going to die with the ship.

With all the men freed, I followed them up to the deck to see them crowded on the starboard side of the ship, away from

Lessie, who was watching them curiously. "Blast it!" one of the sailors cried, his face red with anger. "The lifeboats are gone!"

"What happened here?" I asked them, but the sailors were beside themselves, shouting and yelling as they lamented their ill luck. "We are dead men," the captain moaned, shoving his hands through his silver hair.

Scowling, I looked toward Lessie, who immediately opened her mouth and let out a loud roar. The men instantly quieted, and I used the beat of silence to my advantage. "Let's not get carried away here," I said. "Is there anything we can use on here to make a raft while we go to get you help?"

"Kenrook," Fosse snapped in my ear. "What's going on?"

I ignored him.

The captain glanced up at the mast. "We might be able to topple that."

I frowned. If we were going to start taking the ship apart, we might as well give them something they could sit on. The water was far too cold for them to cling to that mast—they'd last maybe an hour, tops, before they started to catch their death of cold.

"Stand back," I ordered them, gesturing Lessie forward. Using her claws, she broke off a large section of the poop deck, doing her best to keep it intact. At first, the sailors cried out in dismay, but their cries quickly turned to cheers as they realized what Lessie was doing.

The ship chose that moment to groan loudly, rapidly tilting to the right. "Get off the deck!" I cried as we all began sliding. Lessie snatched me just before I slammed into the railing, then tossed me onto her back as she took to the skies. The sudden disappearance of her weight helped stabilize the ship, and the others who hadn't already gone over the edge were able to tie a rope to the railing and shimmy down to the raft waiting below.

"Kenrook," Fosse barked in my ear when Lessie and I circled back around. "We've done more than enough."

"These men could still die out here," I argued as I pulled a rope from my pack. "We need to get them to safety."

"They'll be fine," Fosse countered. "You've made them a nice raft, and a ship is sure to come along eventually. They're commoners, Kenrook, no one of importance. Come back here at once."

Gritting my teeth at his high-handed manner, I ignored my partner and dangled the rope down to the men. "Tie it to the raft!" I shouted, fastening my end to Lessie's pommel. I'd drag them back to the shore if that's what it took to save them.

Sensing my intention, Lessie put on a burst of speed, heading back for the mainland. It was slow going, and I could tell the additional weight was a strain on my poor dragon's muscles, which were not used to bearing such heavy loads. *Mirn could do it,* I thought bitterly as I eyed the larger dragon following us from above. But no, Fosse was going to leave us to flounder here on our own.

I was just starting to worry that I'd have to cut the cord when I spotted a ship coming toward us, flying Elantian colors. The men saw it too, shouting excitedly, and I felt a burst of renewed energy from Lessie as she changed course, heading straight for it.

To my surprise, Fosse and Mirn darted ahead, making a beeline for the ship. I watched as Mirn glided lower so Fosse could speak to the crew, and zoomed in with my goggles to see him pointing to us. The look of frozen politeness on his face told me he was furious, but I was too elated to care. These men were going to be rescued!

The other ship raised its sails, speeding toward us. In no time, it was here, lowering a lifeboat to take in the victims. Relieved, Lessie and I landed on the deck, with the captain's permission, so she could rest her wings a moment and I could find out what happened.

Wrapped in warm blankets, the crew gathered around as the captain of the sunken ship told me how they'd been attacked. It was a bit hard to understand him at first, his teeth were chattering so badly, but someone brought him a cup of rum, and after a few sips, his body relaxed enough for him to speak normally.

"We were attacked by a ship called the *Lora Uwillar* without cause," the captain explained, his voice heating with anger at the memory. "They stole the silver ingots we were carrying, then locked us in the hold and blew a hole in our boat with their cannon. I'm sure they're laughing all the way back to Zallabar now, pleased as punch that they left us to die."

"Zallabar?" I echoed. "How do you know that's where they're from?"

"The accents," one of the other crew members said. "They flew Elantian flags, but they had those thick accents, and they spoke what sounded like Zallabarian to each other."

"You arrived in the nick of time, Miss," the captain said, clasping both his hands in mine. "We really can't thank you enough. My name is Captain Singhold, and my crew and I are in your debt. If there's anything we can ever do to repay you—"

"No need, Captain," I told him with a smile as I stepped back. "I'm just serving my country." Turning to the captain of this ship, I inclined my head. "We appreciate your assistance, Captain Talridge. I'm sure these men will repay you for your kindness."

"It's a pleasure, Miss," the captain said. He and his crew seemed awed to have a dragon on board—they couldn't stop staring at Lessie. "Safe travels to you and your partner."

I thanked him, mounted Lessie again, and took flight. Fosse didn't say a single word as we rejoined him in the sky, but the icy look in his eyes as he held my stare told me he hadn't forgiven me for disobeying him. After several long, uncomfortable seconds, he broke my gaze, and his dragon turned away, heading up the coast again.

"Bizarre," Lessie commented as we continued our patrol. *"Doesn't the military serve the people? Why wouldn't we help those men?"*

"I have no idea," I said, just as bewildered. Fosse's coldness toward his fellow Elantians bothered me almost more than the

Zallabarians who'd attacked them. *"The fact that the Zallabarians were sailing under Elantian colors is something to be concerned about, and we would never have known if we hadn't rescued those men."*

"Do you think this has happened before?" Lessie asked. *"I wonder why Zallabar is sending ships out under false flags when Traggar is the one with the navy."*

"Maybe they've just lent them Zallabarian sailors to do the work," I mused. *"Either way, we need to report this to our superiors so they can start an investigation."*

As we flew over the glittering channel, I scanned the waters for the *Lora Uwillar*, using my goggles to zoom in on Elantian ships and read the names painted on the sides. We needed to do something to protect our ships so this didn't happen again, regardless of whether or not they were military vessels. But we were spread thin as it was, with too few dragons to make much of a difference.

Though the sun continued to shine high in the sky above us, I shivered as a sudden cold whipped through me. How would we be able to prevail against such monstrous people? We kept an eye out for the ship the rest of the day, but found no sign of it, and could only assume that it was long gone, perhaps already returned to the shores from which it came.

If only I knew which shores those were.

17

After Fosse and I returned our dragons to the stable, we went to Colonel Roche's office to give our report. My stomach was heavy with dread as I walked into the room, knowing that Fosse was about to throw me to the wolves.

"Captain, Private," the colonel greeted us. She was sitting behind her desk, and near her shoulder stood Major Duval, the man in charge of the dragon rider contingent. "Report."

I folded my hands behind my back and held in a sigh as Fosse launched right into it. "Nothing out of the ordinary, except that Private Kenrook was insubordinate. She deliberately disobeyed my orders today."

"Oh?" Duval's eyes sharpened as he turned to look at me. I held his gaze but didn't miss the way that Colonel Roche's lips thinned. "What orders were these, Captain?"

"About an hour into our patrol, we ran across a sinking ship," Fosse said. "Kenrook said she wanted to investigate, so she flew down onto the deck while I stayed in the air to keep a lookout. She and her dragon successfully managed to free the crew, who were trapped below decks, and break off a piece of the ship for them to use as a raft."

"That sounds admirable," the major said, raising his eyebrows. The tone in his voice was clear—he failed to see the problem, as did I.

"I agree it was admirable, but she then proceeded to endanger us all by tying the raft to her dragon and towing them to shore," Fosse said, exasperation creeping into his tone. He threw an icy look my way, as if daring me to challenge him, then continued when I said nothing. "It was clear that her dragon wasn't strong enough to pull them all the way to shore, and I didn't want to be stranded out in the open like that, unable to get away quickly if the Traggarans decided to send a warship after us. I ordered Kenrook to leave the raft and return to me, but she refused. Luckily, I flagged down a passing ship and got the men safely aboard before her dragon completely ran out of steam. It was already flagging, and we were barely halfway back," he sneered.

My cheeks stung as three sets of disapproving eyes swung my way, but I refused to back down. "Permission to speak?" I asked stiffly.

The colonel held my gaze for a long moment. "Granted."

"It's true that I disobeyed orders," I said, keeping my tone unhurried even though the words wanted to rush out of me. "But those men needed help, and I needed a safe place to interrogate them. Their ship started to sink before I could finish asking them questions, so I brought them to a safer place where I could. They claim their ship was attacked and looted by Zallabarians."

The colonel sat up straighter in her chair. "What proof do you have of this?" she demanded.

"None but their statements," I told her. "They say that the other ship was flying Elantian colors, but that the crew spoke Zallabarian to each other, and had thick Zallabarian accents. The enemy ship was called the *Lora Uwillar*, and the crew stole a large number of silver ingots, then blew a hole in the side of the ship and locked the other crew in the hold before leaving them there to die."

"That is concerning," Major Duval said, his forehead furrowing. "Did you see any sign of this enemy ship?"

"No," I admitted. "I searched, but it was long gone. Even so, I believe they were telling the truth."

"And how can you know that for sure?" the colonel asked sharply. "They could have been flying false colors, just like this imaginary ship they claimed attacked them. A ship that you yourself could not find after hours of searching."

"They were *Elantian natives*," I fired back, infuriated by her condescending tone. "And I'm sure they didn't decide to blow a hole in their own ship and lock themselves in the cargo hold for fun. We saved nine lives today and gathered valuable intelligence in the process. Captain Fosse here might not think those lives matter"—I jabbed a finger in my partner's direction—"but the common people deserve our help just as much as anyone else. Given the chance, I would do it again in a heartbeat."

Major Duval stared at me with what looked suspiciously like respect, but Colonel Roche was having none of it. "Enough!" She slapped her hand on her desk, her face ruddy. "I warned you about insubordination, Private," she seethed, "and yet here you are, flaunting your disobedience in my face. The fact that it ended well is not an excuse. As Captain Fosse says, you put both of your dragons in danger with your actions. As of right now, you and Lessie are grounded for the next two days, and I will be filing a reprimand for insubordination. Is that understood?"

"Yes, ma'am," I said through gritted teeth.

"Good. You are dismissed."

Turning on my heel, I strode out of the building, refusing to look at my gloating partner. He was getting off on this, but I wouldn't give him the satisfaction of an acknowledgment. Keeping my steps measured, I headed to the mess hall for dinner. I was starving and hoped a hot meal would take the edge off my temper.

Grounded. For two days. Because I did the right thing.

I was so pissed off at the injustice of it all that I didn't see Jallis and ran right into him. "Hey!" He grabbed my shoulders, and I jerked back. "You okay?" he asked, trying to peer into my eyes.

"Peachy," I growled, stepping past him. I snatched up a tray and slid into line, not in the mood to deal with him. But naturally, this was the day he decided to flout convention and sidle up next to me.

"You're fuming so hot I can see the steam rising out of your ears," he murmured behind me.

"How nice of you to notice," I said.

I could hear the frown in his voice. "What's going on? Why are you being so rude to me?"

Spinning around, I lowered my voice to a hiss. "Why don't you do what you're supposed to do, and scurry back to your officer friends before they see you slumming it with me?" He jerked back, as if I'd slapped him, and the way his face paled with shock gave me no small amount of perverse satisfaction. "After all, we do what's expected of us around here, not what's right, don't we?"

Swearing under his breath, Jallis held up his hands to give me some space. "I don't know what's going on, but you and I are going to talk later," he said in a low voice that sent a shiver up my spine.

"You're not the boss of me," I said in an equally low voice, aware that I was being petulant.

He raised an eyebrow. "I outrank you."

Thanks for the reminder, I almost said, but it was my turn. Handing the woman behind the counter my tray, I kept my eyes on her as I ignored the stares. I knew my little spat with Jallis had drawn attention, but I didn't care.

The woman handed me back something that vaguely resembled stew, and I took it away, leaving Jallis behind to order his own food. Kade, Ullion, and Daria waved, but I only gave them a small nod as I walked past. Their curious looks followed me all the way to the empty table in the corner of the hall, and I squashed a tiny pinprick of guilt at ditching them. Normally I was more than happy to sit with them—as the oldest of us, I felt a responsibility to stick by them—but today, I just wanted to eat my food and be left alone.

Jallis walked away from the counter with his food, and I held my breath as his eyes locked with mine. Was he going to come and sit with me? Time seemed to suspend for a brief moment, and then he looked away, heading toward his usual table.

"Of course he's not going to sit with you," I muttered sullenly. Jallis wasn't going to risk alienating himself from the other officers just because I was having a shitty day. Maybe it was selfish of me to expect him to, since he'd already risked so much for me. He'd been working toward this his entire life. But the fact that he'd taken such a giant step back from me hurt more than I cared to admit.

Suddenly, I had no desire to be in the same room as Jallis, breathing the same air. Ducking my head, I shoveled down my food as quickly as possible, then left the mess hall, heading out into the warm evening air.

"Zara." Lessie's consciousness brushed up against mine, full of concern. *"Are you okay?"*

No. I wasn't okay. I was a boiling, seething mass of fury, and at this moment I wished I were a dragon so I could open my mouth and release my anger in a torrent of flame. I'd also settle for punching Fosse in his stupid, self-righteous face, if he were around. Of course, that would get me into even more trouble, so maybe that wasn't such a good idea.

I really wasn't cut out for this military stuff, was I?

"I'm okay," I said to Lessie, not wanting her to worry. Knowing she could feel my volatile emotions, I added, *"I just need to take a walk, cool off for a bit. I'll come snuggle with you later."*

"Okay." She gave me one of those mind-nuzzles that felt like she was rubbing up against me even though she wasn't actually here. *"Be safe, Zara."*

I nodded, even though she couldn't see me, and checked to make sure my weapons were still on me. I had my military-issued sword, my daggers, and my dragon blade on me. The crossbow, also military-issue, I'd left behind in the barracks—it was great for when I was on dragonback, but too bulky to carry around.

Still, I knew being armed wasn't enough, not where Salcombe was concerned, so I made sure to stick close to the buildings as I walked, remaining in sight of the windows.

It didn't take long for Jallis to fall into step with me. He said nothing as we walked together in the dying sunlight, grass and dirt rustling beneath our feet. But I could feel his questioning glances as he waited for me to break.

"Aren't you worried someone's going to see you with me?" I finally asked, though I still didn't turn to look at him.

Jallis sighed. "You've had a rough day, and you need a friend," he said. "That's more important than the rules. I just wish you'd tell me what's going on so I'm not out here breaking them for nothing."

I glanced sharply at him. "Is that what spending time with me is, then? Nothing?"

Jallis threw up his hands. "You can't blame me for toeing the line, Zara. You made it clear that you weren't sure if you wanted to be more than friends, so I'm not about to risk my position when you're not certain of yours."

His words were like a slap to the face, and I stopped so suddenly he had to double back. "I'm still your friend, Zara," he said quietly. "We might not be allowed to hang out together, but you can still come to me if you're in trouble."

I looked up into Jallis's eyes, which were wide with sincerity. Damn, I was an idiot. Of course Jallis was keeping his distance. He wasn't going to stick his neck out for me when I wasn't sure I wanted to offer him more than a dalliance. And I was a terrible person for expecting him to.

"Lessie and I have been grounded," I said tightly. "For two days. And I have a permanent mark on my record, all because I refused to leave a stranded crew to die."

Jallis fell into step beside me again, and as we walked, I told him the whole story. I expected him to be just as outraged as I felt about the injustice of it all, but when I finished, he was frowning thoughtfully, gazing out into the twilight.

"Well?" I demanded. "Aren't you going to say anything?"

He shook his head. "Sorry. Just trying to organize my thoughts."

He gave me a sympathetic smile. "I wouldn't worry about the reprimand, Zara. The kind of people who get things done, the ones willing to take risks and get their hands dirty, are always going to get a few slaps on the wrist along the way. Rhia and I got reprimands when we left Dragon's Table to rescue you without permission."

I blinked. "I thought you said nothing happened."

He shrugged. "We didn't want you to feel guilty about it. I don't regret what I did, and I'd do it again in a heartbeat. What you did today, saving those men, was admirable, and shows great courage and heart. I'm happy nothing went wrong, and that you even got some good intelligence."

"I sense a 'but' coming," I said dryly.

"*But,*" Jallis continued, deliberately emphasizing the word as he raised his eyebrows at me, "Fosse was right to dress you down for it. He was wrong to tell you those men weren't worth saving merely because they were commoners, but the fact remains that Lessie is worth a hundred human lives in the eyes of our superiors, especially now that we're on the verge of war."

"Are you serious?" I gaped at him. "If that's the case, then why are we fighting at all, if the dragons are so much more precious than human lives? Why not just lock them away?"

Jallis pinched the bridge of his nose. "I'm just telling you how the others think. Whether you like it or not, Major Duval is going to keep a very close eye on you now, and any further instances of insubordination are going to be punished much more harshly. You need to be careful, Zara."

I gnashed my teeth, my hands itching to clench into fists. I knew Jallis was right, but his words still stung. I expected a sympathetic ear, and instead he sided with Fosse and the others, who'd refused to acknowledge the value of the intelligence I'd brought back.

"This is ridiculous," I fumed. "First you go telling me that it's okay to take risks, and now you're telling me I was wrong for doing exactly that. I trusted my gut, Jallis, and it paid off bigtime. How am I supposed to do my job if I have to ignore my instincts like this?"

"You don't have to do it forever!" Jallis barked, surprising me. His eyes glittered with annoyance as he leaned in, lowering his voice so we wouldn't be overheard. "You just need to do it long enough until you get promoted! You and Lessie are a talented pair, and no rider gets stuck as a private for long. If you'd just follow orders and keep your head down, you'll get promoted to officer and you'll have more leeway. And then we won't have to keep skulking about like this!"

"What if I don't want to be an officer?" I hissed. "What if I don't want to be in the military, period?"

Jallis's green eyes iced over as he stepped back. "You should have thought of that before you picked up Lessie's egg, then."

He turned away, his shoulders stiff with anger, and I grabbed his wrist. "Wait," I begged, torn between guilt and anger. Why couldn't I seem to keep it together today? "I'm sorry, Jallis. I didn't mean for it to come out like that. It's just...you've had your whole life to prepare for a military career. I haven't, and

I'm not bred for this. My entire life I've learned how to live in a world where the rules are flexible at best, and now I have to readjust to a strict hierarchy where every move I make has to be approved by someone else. I want to help protect our country, but I don't think I can keep doing this when these judgmental superior officers are determined to squash every good idea I have."

Jallis turned back to face me, his expression softening. "I'm sorry, Zara. I know this is hard for you. But people end up in the military all the time who have little training or experience, and they have to suck it up. Everyone pays their dues when they first get here. Once you pay yours and finally start settling into your role, things will get easier." He glanced over his shoulder. "I have to get back now."

"Go," I said with a sigh, waving him away. He seemed apologetic, so I didn't want to give him too much of a hard time. "I guess I'll see you around if I ever get that mythical promotion."

He gave me a crooked smile. "I have no doubt that you will," he said softly.

With Jallis gone, I made my way to the stables, seeking out Lessie for comfort. As we snuggled in the hay together, I told her about the meeting, and our punishment.

"Grounded?" She bristled indignantly. *"What is that supposed to mean?"*

"It means that we can't fly for two days," I said heavily.

"How are we supposed to go on patrol if we can't fly?"

"*We're not.*" I smiled wryly. "*I guess you can say this is a little vacation.*"

"*Vacation.*" She huffed. "*That's one way to look at it.*"

The next morning, after breakfast, I asked Major Duval what Lessie and I would be doing over the next two days, since we were stuck on the ground. "Study up on your Traggaran and review this book on military rules and regs." He handed me a small, leather-bound book. "You may also take your dragon out for walks and runs, as it is important for you both to keep your fitness up."

That last bit perked me right up, and I immediately fetched Lessie from the stables. As long as the two of us stuck together, it was perfectly safe to go exploring in daylight, and I'd been itching to learn more about the terrain.

Lessie was in the middle of breakfast when I arrived, but she wolfed down the rest of her raw mutton and eagerly joined me. Not wanting to alarm the officers, who'd already informed me I'd been grounded, I waited until we were clear of the camp before I jumped on her back.

"*It's been a long time since we've run around like this,*" Lessie said as she galloped through the meadows, heading for the nearby beech woods. As we passed through the tree line, Lessie tucked her wings in tight. "*It's not as good as flying, but it does clear the head.*"

"*I agree,*" I said, jumping down to the ground so I could get some exercise as well. Lessie slowed to match my speed, and together we ran at a leisurely pace alongside a brook, soaking in the sights and smells of the forest. The sound of twittering birds, the dappled sunlight illuminating the bushes and roots sticking out of the ground, the smell of blossoming flowers...all these things were as familiar to me as my lock picks and gear, a balm to my soul.

Out of old habit, I scanned the area with my treasure sense. If Salcombe and his men were here, it would pick up on any weapons or equipment they carried. I didn't sense anything like that, but I did pick up on a few underground burial chambers beneath a few hillocks. Part of me itched to seek them out, but since I was stuck here, with no safe place to store the treasure, I refrained. Besides, I didn't like disturbing new graves, and judging by the contents buried within these, they were only a few decades old.

Eventually, Lessie and I tired ourselves out, and we made our way back to camp, feeling far more relaxed. *"Do you think I could use my treasure sense against the enemy?"* I asked Lessie as I sat astride her.

"In what way?"

"I dunno." I shrugged. *"The Traggaran soldiers and sailors must be paid and supplied. I could use my treasure sense to locate and raid their cash reserves and disrupt their operations. That would definitely spread discontent when the soldiers start going hungry, and maybe even rebellion."*

"It's not a bad idea," Lessie said. *"If we did it on a foggy night, as I suggested, I could sneak you in easily without being spotted myself. But do you think you could get such a mission approved?"*

I sighed. *"Probably not."* If the recent disaster with Fosse had taught me anything, it was that the officers had very little imagination and wouldn't listen to suggestions from a lowly private like me. I could try to put the idea in Jallis's head, see if he could get some traction for it, but I didn't feel like talking to him right now.

The moment Lessie and I reentered the military camp, a heavy weight settled on my shoulders. Judgmental looks followed us as I returned to the barracks to study, as Major Duval suggested, and I decided right then and there that I would get out of the military at the first opportunity. I wouldn't desert, of course, but I'd start scouring the books for any legal loophole I could find. I was never cut out for being a cog in a giant machine like this, and neither was Lessie. If we wanted to make our mark on the world, we were going to have to find another way.

18

The two-day punishment passed fairly quickly, and in no time at all, Lessie and I were back in the air again. Fosse, to my relief, had been reassigned to another partner, so I was patrolling with Trylon Carvis, one of the older riders who had been called from the reserves. He too held the rank of captain, and was just as stubborn as Fosse. But his wasn't the stubbornness of an ambitious officer trying to throw his weight around. No, Carvis was merely an old dog, too tired and set in his ways to learn new tricks.

Thankfully, Carvis's dragon, Hallus, was hardier, and he seemed happy to be flying again. Unlike Mirn, Fosse's dragon, he actually got along with Lessie, and I could tell by her cheerful demeanor that the two of them conversed together even though Carvis himself treated me with the same reserved silence as all the other older riders.

The first few days of our patrol were fairly uneventful—we had intermittent rain followed by bursts of sunshine that kept us on our toes, but no suspicious activity drew our attention. In fact, flying up and down the same stretch of coast, seeing the same thing day after day, became somewhat tedious. By the fourth morning, I wished I could switch places with Rhia at the Zallabarian border, if only to get the chance to see something *different*.

On the fifth day, however, something was different. I woke up with an itch in the back of my skull, and tension gripped my shoulders as Lessie and I took to the skies with Carvis and Hallus. I scanned the skies and the sea, searching for anything out of place, but for the first two hours, everything was as it should be.

And then I saw it.

"Captain?" I called, pointing to the horizon. Just a moment ago, the sky had been perfectly normal, but thick clouds, tall as towering mountains, were rolling in at an alarming rate. "Is that one of those sudden storms we've been warned about?"

"They're just clouds," he said shortly.

"Just clouds?" I echoed with disbelief. "But—"

"We have orders, Private," Carvis barked, cutting me off. "We're staying the course."

Hallus, his dull yellow scales glinting in the afternoon light, tossed his head nervously. I could tell he wasn't thrilled about flying into what looked like a nasty storm, but he had to obey his rider, and I had to follow orders. Gritting my teeth, I seriously considered the idea of leaving his dumb ass and heading back to camp. But I didn't want to get slapped with another reprimand, and there was still time for Carvis to come to his senses and turn back.

"Hallus says if the storm gets too bad, he will turn back regardless of what Carvis says," Lessie tried to assure me. *"Their bond is old and very strong, so it is difficult for him to resist Carvis's commands, but he can do it if absolutely necessary."*

"Okay." Holding in a sigh, I leaned into Lessie as we banked left. We were supposed to be checking on the build-up of hostile ships at Raistin, the southern port that Jallis had mentioned was building an armada. Usually, this was only done at night, but today was overcast, and safe enough that Lessie and I would be able to get close enough to do a count. The clouds from the incoming storm might be helpful in that regard...if it didn't kill us first.

Ten minutes later, we were hovering above the Traggaran coast, high enough that we'd be hard to spot. Flying over the port, I adjusted my goggles to zoom in and get a proper look. But before I could, two large clouds surrounded us, blocking my view completely.

"Captain!" I shouted, looking around for Hallus and Carvis. They had hung back a few hundred yards, since the larger dragon would be easier to see. "Are you all right?"

"I can't see a blasted thing!" he shouted back, just as hail started to pepper us. Swearing, I immediately hunkered down on Lessie's back and covered my head with my arms to protect it. Most of the hailstones were small, the size of my pinky, but there were some alarmingly large ones, and I cried out in pain as one struck my shoulder.

"Hallus says we need to leave now," Lessie said, turning around. *"But I can't figure out which way is south!"*

Lightning arced through the sky, followed by an ear-splitting roar of pain from Hallus. My heart leaped into my throat as the clouds parted, and I saw dragon and rider hurtling toward the ocean.

"NO!" I screamed as thunder crashed around my ears. Lessie tucked her wings in and dove for the ocean, hurtling through the sky as she tried to get to Carvis. But the heavier dragon was falling too fast, and he hit the sea long before we could reach him.

"Up!" I cried, as a massive wave, created by the impact, rolled toward us. Lessie pumped her wings hard to get us clear, then screeched as a gale wind buffeted us. I held on for dear life as we tumbled through the sky, hail and wind battering me from every angle. Several long, terror-filled minutes passed before Lessie was able to right herself again.

"Head for land!" I shouted, pointing to the island ahead. It wasn't the same island we'd been flying over before—this was the island of Inna Mar, the largest of the Traggaran islands and home to the capital, Puilin.

Lessie did her best, but the wind and hail continued to pummel her, making the descent extremely difficult. Gripping the pommel, I tried not to let fear get to me, but it was far too easy to imagine us getting dashed against the rocky cliffs as we hovered low, trying to find a safe place to land. We'd managed to avoid being struck by lightning, like poor Hallus, but we weren't out of the woods by a long shot.

Finally, Lessie managed to land on a hill with an old castle ruin at the top, with walls large enough to provide cover from anyone who might be able to see us. I nearly cried in relief when she touched down, but I managed to hold it together—she was in great pain, and she needed me.

"He's dead," Lessie wailed as she rolled onto her side, seconds after I dismounted. *"He was just in the middle of telling me which way to go when that lightning struck him!"*

"Shhh!" I hissed, rushing to her side. I wrapped my arms around her neck and stroked her, trying to silence her screeches of pain and grief. "It's not safe here! Someone might hear you and come to investigate."

Lessie quieted immediately, but I could still feel her pain, raw and fresh. It was like a punch to the gut, and tears of sympathy pricked at my own eyes. I didn't have much love for Carvis, but his dragon had been innocent in all this. The fact that he'd died because his rider had been too stubborn and stupid to turn back infuriated me more than anything else.

"Let's have a look at you," I murmured, running my hands along Lessie's body. Her scales were fine—it took more than hail to pierce a dragon's hide—but her wings were badly damaged. There was a small hole in the left wing, and strained tendons and muscles in both.

Swearing, I unstrapped my crossbow and pack from my back,

then rummaged through the latter looking for supplies. There wasn't much I could do, but I broke off some branches from a nearby tree and used them, along with some twine from my pack, to create a kind of brace for the pulled muscle. The tear in the left wing I slathered with ointment, then taped over with a bandage.

"I'm sorry, Lessie," I said when I was finished. She was lying on her belly, her wings spread out, looking miserable. *"I wish I could do more."*

"It's fine," she said, though I could tell it wasn't. *"This will all heal in a few days."*

I stroked her snout. *"I'm going to go get you some food. Wait here for me."*

She snorted. *"As if I can go anywhere."*

My lips twitched, pleased to see some of her snarky personality coming back. With my crossbow in hand and weapons strapped to my sides, I headed down the hill and into the forest, searching for game to bring down.

Three hours later, I came back, dragging a young trozla and a brace of rabbits. Moving indoors to what was left of the great hall, Lessie devoured the larger animal while I roasted the rabbits over a fire I'd built in the hearth. The two of us sat silently in the deserted hall, thinking.

"You want to track down Red Beard," Lessie finally said.

I sighed. *"I want to do something useful. Patrolling the border when no one will listen to our suggestions or allow us to take any action isn't useful. The two of us could have been killed today."*

The thought still gripped me with terror every time it entered my mind, and I tried to push it away. But Lessie curled her neck around me, comforting me with the warmth and weight of her body.

"I was terrified," she confessed. *"Now that we are here, I understand why you were so apprehensive about going to war. When that gale wind hit me, and I was struggling in the air, I was scared you were going to fall off and end up in the ocean with Hallus and Carvis. In fact, I'm amazed you managed to stay on."*

I smiled, wrapping an arm around her. *"It'll take more than a bit of wind to separate us."*

The two of us fell asleep in the hall together, both of us too exhausted to set a watch. The next morning, I went out again to hunt for more food, wanting to keep Lessie supplied with meat. The more she ate, the faster she'd heal, and the sooner we could fly out of here.

I was following a set of boar tracks when I heard voices.

"I'm telling you, there ain't no dragon out in these parts," a man grumbled in Traggaran. "You musta been seein' things."

"I wasn't imaginin' it!" another man protested. "I saw it, a big, shiny blue one!"

Holding my breath, I pressed my back against a large tree trunk, listening. I couldn't make out everything they were saying, but I understood enough. The second man who'd spoken had dragged out the other men, looking for Lessie. He thought that if the three of them could capture or kill her, they'd get a nice, fat reward from the town mayor. Maybe even recognition from the king.

The men passed right by my hiding place, and I counted heads. One, two, three, four, five. All armed with bows and swords.

Too many to take on hand-to-hand. But I couldn't let them reach Lessie.

The moment the men were out of sight, I sprinted from my hiding place and headed straight for the hill, using an alternate route to the one the men were on. Luckily, they'd chosen the long way around, and I managed to beat them back to the castle.

"What's wrong?" Lessie asked as I raced inside.

"We're under attack." I eyed my dragon as she lurched to her feet. *"Can you fly?"*

"We might be able to in another day or so," Lessie said. *"But—"*

"Not we." I cut her off. *"Can you fly? If you didn't have any weight, not even the saddle?"*

Lessie drew herself upright, her eyes blazing. *"Absolutely not,"* she said. *"I am not leaving you behind on this forsaken island—"* She broke off, lifting her head. *"I hear them. They're coming."*

Swearing, I raced past her, up the stairs, to the tallest tower. Sure enough, the men were coming, weapons drawn. They were burly and mean-looking, and outnumbered me five to one.

But these men didn't have a castle. Or a dragon.

"*Stay silent,*" I ordered Lessie, sensing her intent. She wanted to rush out there and spew fire all over these dragon-killing bastards, and I didn't blame her. "*Let me try to kill these assholes before they, or anyone who might be watching, can confirm you're here.*"

"*Fine,*" Lessie relented. "*But if they make it to the walls, I'm going after them.*"

"*I expect nothing less.*"

Knowing I didn't have much time, I stuck my foot in the stirrup of my crossbow and yanked the string across the barrel. Sweat beaded on my forehead as I loaded a bolt into the barrel and lifted the crossbow so the sight was at eye-level.

Bow and arrow had never been my strength, but I'd gotten better since joining the academy. I'd even learned to bring down game with them, thanks to Tavarian's training.

But this would be my first time bringing down a human.

Using the sight, I aimed, seeking out the closest man. Black hair, with a scar across his cheek. *Center mass,* I told myself, aiming for his chest.

I pulled in a deep breath, let out half of it. Paused. And pulled the trigger.

The bolt exploded from the crossbow, zipping across the field. It didn't hit the center of his chest, like I'd expected, but I got him in the gut, and he screamed, stumbling back. The other men cried out in alarm, and I hurriedly re-cocked my bow.

One of the men tried to shoot at me with his own bow, but his arrow bounced harmlessly off the castle walls, too far away to make it to my tower. Gritting my teeth, I lifted the bow again, aimed. Fired.

Missed the chest again, but got the second guy right in the throat.

He fell to his knees, clutching at the arrow embedded in his neck as he bled out.

The other three men started shouting in Traggaran, but I didn't bother to try and decipher what they were saying. I loaded my crossbow, lifted it. The men raced away, leaving their comrades as they fled down the hill.

I managed to shoot one in the back before the other two disappeared.

"Zara?" Lessie asked. *"Are you all right?"*

"I'm fine." I cocked my crossbow again, trained it on the man I'd shot in the gut. He was struggling to his feet, trying to chase after the comrades who had left him without a thought. My second arrow found his heart, and this time when he went down, he stayed down.

Good riddance.

I cocked my crossbow one more time, then just stood there, my weapon trained on the hill, waiting to see if those men would reappear. After a few minutes, I swiveled around, checking to make sure they hadn't decided to sneak up the back to have another go at me.

Finally, I came down.

"You're shaking," Lessie said, her eyes round with concern as I entered the hall, my crossbow disarmed. Tossing it aside, I rushed over to her, throwing my arms around her neck.

"You need to leave. Tonight."

Lessie stiffened. *"I won't abandon you, Zara."*

"You're not abandoning me. You're saving us both." I pulled back to look into her fiery eyes. *"We can't wait around here for you to heal enough to carry us both back. Those three men might come back. If you're able to fly, you need to get out of here as soon as the sun sets."*

"But where will I go?" Lessie cried plaintively. My heart ached at the pain and confusion I felt from her. *"And what will you do?"*

"You'll go back to base, wait for me. And I'll seek out Tavarian," I decided. *"He's our best bet for getting out of this stupid war so we can focus on Salcombe, and he's all alone in enemy territory. If he's still on the island, I want to do whatever I can to help him."*

Lessie sighed. *"The capital is on the other side of the island, over a hundred and fifty miles from here. And you don't know that he's still on the island"*

I shrugged. *"I can walk that in a few days. It's only been two weeks since Tavarian left for Traggar from Dragon's Table, and it took him longer than that to deal with Quoronis, who aren't nearly as difficult as the Traggarans. If he's not at the capital, I'll just make my way to the port and barter passage back to Elantia. It's far easier to travel by ship from that side of the island anyway, since it's directly facing the channel."*

I also wouldn't have to deal with Colonel Roche or any of the other bigwigs back at camp. That alone was worth spending a few days in enemy territory.

"Walk." Lessie huffed. *"You're a dragon rider. You shouldn't have to walk."* I could feel her guilt at not being able to carry me, at running away while I stayed behind and put myself in danger.

Smiling, I laid my cheek against hers and looked into one of her great, fiery eyes. *"I'd walk to the ends of the world for you."*

Lessie chuffed with laughter. *"That is the tritest thing you've ever said to me,"* she said. *"But I can tell you mean it."*

"Of course I do." I grinned as I snuggled against her as best I could. *"We're soulmates. Together forever, no matter what."*

19

Once I was certain the men were gone, I ventured out to get Lessie more food to prepare her for the long flight. Unwilling to go too far, I stuck to the edges of the woods, and eventually came back with three rabbits and two large red-and-blue feathered birds.

I thought Lessie would complain about the meager fare, but she ate it without complaint, then immediately settled down to snuggle with me. We sat there in the hall, enjoying the companionable silence, keeping our ears and minds alert as we waited for the sun to set.

Neither of us wanted to admit it, but we knew this could very well end up being the last time we ever saw each other.

When the last of the sun's rays finally disappeared from the sky, I led Lessie out. Her wings were still dragging a bit, but they looked much better than they had yesterday. I hoped the splints would help the wings bear her weight.

"We don't have to do this," Lessie said for the umpteenth time, even as she flexed her wings. *"We can try to stick this out together."*

"No," I said gently. *"We can't."*

Lessie gave her wings a few experimental flaps, then leaped into the air. Relief mingled with sadness as I watched her do a few laps around the castle. A bit shaky, but far smoother than I expected.

She landed in front of me, and I put on a brave smile for her. *"You're good to go."*

Lessie curled her neck around me, and we hugged one last time. *"Be careful, Zara,"* she said. *"I'll never forgive myself if something happens to you."*

"I will," I promised. After all, anything that happened to me, also happened to her. And I refused to let Lessie suffer for any reason.

As Lessie took off into the night, I briefly wished I had Tavarian's magic so I could cloak her the way he did with Muza. But Lessie had plenty of experience with stealth flying, and so long as her wings held her up, she would be able to stay hidden in the sky.

I just hoped she had enough strength in her to make it across the channel.

Wiping away tears, I headed back inside for a few hours of sleep. But knowing those men were out there prevented me from being able to truly relax, and instead I ended up prepping for the trip. I stripped off my telltale riding leathers and hid both them and the crossbow in an old, musty crate I found in a storage chamber. Both items would give me away immediately, as well as my uniform tunic, but the shirt I wore beneath, combined with the pants, was fairly inconspicuous. Rummaging through my pack, I removed anything else that might identify me as an Elantian, including the coins in my money pouch. It was a shame to have to leave them behind, but they were stamped with the Elantian crest, so I couldn't be caught carrying them. Luckily, I had three silvers that were worn out, and I did tuck those into one of my pockets. Hopefully, I'd be able to get a few warm meals out of them.

I repacked my bag, making sure my goggles and lock pick were tucked away safely. My knives were tucked into my boots and belt, and I strapped the dragon blade to my belt as well, short-ening it so much that it looked more like a double-bladed knife than anything else.

And then I sat, and waited.

When the sun finally peeked her head over the horizon, I stood, more than ready to get on with the journey. Squaring my shoul-ders, I headed out, down the hill and through a winding path in the forest. My military-issue compass proved handy in telling me which way to go, and I quietly hummed a tune under my breath to try to keep my spirits up.

The forest seemed to go on forever—I knew from the brief scouting I'd done from one of the castle towers that the trees spread out for miles, almost as far as the eye could see. I didn't think I would run across any troops, but just in case, I kept my senses open, including my treasure sense.

I managed eight miles before I had to stop and rest, my legs burning from the exertion. Resting underneath a large tree, I pulled out the remnants of the roasted rabbit from last night and ate, wishing that the hard ground beneath me was a soft bed I could lay my head on.

You're getting soft, I scolded myself. Before coming to the dragon rider academy, I'd been well used to sleeping on the ground with only my bedroll to soften the dirt beneath me. While I did carry small, lightweight tents on my expeditions, I didn't bring mattresses or pads since they were just unnecessary weight.

Now, though, I wasn't looking forward to sleeping on the cold, hard ground. I missed my bed. I missed my dragon. Hell, I even missed Jallis, despite my anger at the way he'd treated me.

It could be way worse, I told myself. Lessie and I could have been killed by lightning. I could have fallen and suffered amnesia. Some soldiers could come upon me and string me up as a spy.

I winced at that last one, which was still likely to happen. I needed to get myself some less conspicuous clothing, something that would make me blend in with the natives. I was pretty sure Traggaran women didn't wear trousers.

I allowed myself thirty minutes' rest before pushing on. My treasure sense picked up items here and there, but aside from a small cache of coins I found buried beneath a tree root, most of the items were too large for me to carry.

The sun was high in the sky when I finally made it out of the woods, and I drew in a deep breath of fresh, clean air as I stepped into a meadow. Feeling far more optimistic about my chances of finding an inn for the night, I quickened my pace, ignoring the blisters forming on my heels.

It only took two more hours of walking before I spotted my first sign of civilization—an isolated farm. The sound of cows mooing and chickens clucking lifted my spirits. When I saw a blonde woman wearing a brown dress and white apron walking toward the house, carrying what looked like a pail of milk, it took everything I had not to run right up to her.

Instead, I approached at a casual pace, giving her a friendly smile. "Hello," I said in Traggaran when the woman saw me, her eyes flying wide. "Can I trouble you for some help?"

The woman glanced around, seeming nervous, but I did my best to sound as non-threatening as possible as I conversed with her in broken Traggaran, hoping she wouldn't pick up that I was Elantian. Eventually, we managed to come to an understanding, and she invited me into the house—in exchange for two of my silvers, she would sell me one of her dresses, and throw in a meal for free.

Grateful, I sat down at her table and scarfed down a meal of cheese, bread, and eggs while she fetched the dress. She came back down with a dark green outfit that, while a little baggy in the chest and hips, fit well enough. She offered me shoes, too, but I declined—my boots would be easier to conceal my knives in. For a third silver, she allowed me to sleep in the barn loft, and though I missed Lessie terribly, I eventually managed to drift off to the gentle sound of mooing cows below.

The next morning, I continued my journey, my spirits somewhat improved by the food and rest. Halfway through the day, I made it to the main road to the capital, wider and more worn than the road I'd previously traveled on. I had a lot more company, and I decided the extended dragon blade would draw too much attention.

Spying an oxcart loaded up with bales of hay, I ran up alongside it and held up a coin. The driver's eyes glittered with suspicion, but using hand signals to communicate, I managed to convince him I was deaf and dumb and no threat to him. After a minute, he took the coin and allowed me to climb up into the cart and settle in amongst the hay.

Finally, I thought, stretching out my weary legs. I leaned my head back against one of the hay bales, ignoring the bits of dried grass poking into my neck as I tried to get some sleep. Reaching through the bond, I reassured myself that Lessie was still okay. I sensed that she'd made it back across the channel, though she was too far away to talk to. I missed her fiercely and sincerely hoped I'd find Tavarian so I could get back to her soon.

Why did Carvis have to be so stupid? I grumbled. If he hadn't stubbornly insisted on flying into that storm, Lessie and I would be back at the camp. As far as I was concerned, military discipline was more of a hindrance than a help. Maybe it worked just fine for green recruits, but I was an experienced treasure hunter and I knew how to scout and canvas from my old thieving days. If I ever made it back to Elantia, I resolved never again to blindly follow orders, no matter who they came from. I refused to risk Lessie's life again on the say-so of another dragon rider, even if he was higher ranked.

Eventually, I fell asleep, but it felt like only seconds before I was rudely awakened again by the sensation of someone's fingers digging into my bicep. Opening my eyes, I expected to see the driver, but my mouth dropped open at the sight of a city guard, his eyes glittering with malice.

"Let me go!" I shrieked, kicking him in the stomach.

He stumbled back with a shout, and the carter, who was standing nearby, smirked. "See! I told you she was lying! She's no mute. She's an Elantian spy!"

"Shit!" I must have shouted in my native tongue when the guard grabbed me. Springing to my feet, I raced in the opposite direction, jumping on the backs of the oxen. They mooed loudly as I spring-boarded off their heads, grabbed the edge of an awning, and pulled myself up onto a thatched roof.

"After her!" someone shrieked, and I put on a burst of speed. My footsteps made no sound as I raced across the rooftops—if anyone was inside these buildings, they'd never know I was running above their heads. Unfortunately, it was still daylight, making me far too visible to those on the streets. All it would take was someone with good aim...

An arrow whizzed by my head, as if on cue, and I hissed as it cut my cheek. Swearing, I swung down from the roof, dropped into the street, and dashed into an alley. My breath sawed in my lungs as I zigged and zagged through the warren of streets, glancing over my shoulder constantly to see if I was still being followed. Eventually, I managed to lose the guards, but as a precaution I climbed another building and jimmied open the window so I could hide in the attic.

That was way too close.

Shaking my head, I leaned against one of the dusty boxes and cocked my ear, listening to the commotion outside. After that debacle, there was no way I was going to let my guard down enough to fall asleep. What had I been thinking? That asshole driver must have pegged me as a foreigner and turned me in. I had no idea which town I was in, but I hadn't been traveling long enough to have reached the capital. I needed to get out of here and keep moving.

Rummaging through the attic boxes, I found an old, off-white cloth and wrapped it around my head, tucking my red curls under it to hide them. I had a feeling my hair had tipped off the carter—it wasn't a common color. Once I was sure that my hair was properly covered, I waited until the hubbub outside died down, then quietly slipped out of the city and into the nearby fields.

I wonder if this was a giant mistake, I thought glumly as I trudged through the tall grass. My broken Traggaran and lack of knowledge were both giant handicaps in a place like this—it was going to be very hard to blend in, and even harder to find Tavarian in the capital once I was there without drawing attention to my foreignness. Perhaps it would have been safer to stay with Lessie until her wings were healed, then fly back across the channel together at the first opportunity.

But in my heart, I knew that wasn't true. Those men would have returned with reinforcements, and Lessie and I would have been captured. It was far safer to send her back on her own. Besides, I couldn't help but feel that returning to camp was a bad idea. What if my superior officer sent Lessie and me on another fool-hardy mission, one that actually *did* get us killed? Surely if I could find Tavarian and explain what happened, he'd figure out a way to get us out of this situation so we could get back to tracking down the other pieces of the dragon god's heart. Lessie and I didn't belong in the military. We belonged with Tavarian.

The moment I thought the words, a sense of rightness clicked into place. I didn't know how exactly, or why, but my gut told me that Lessie and I would do the most good at Tavarian's side. Everything good that had happened in our lives was because of him.

I crested a hill, my mood lifting as I saw a small town up ahead. Glancing around to make sure no one was nearby, I dug the silver coins I'd found in the woods out of my pack and counted. I had enough here to feed myself for a couple of weeks, plus buy a better outfit. This peasant garb wasn't going to cut it—peasants and farmers would be expected to know the local language, and I didn't.

Heading into town, I stopped at a dressmaker and bought myself one of the pre-made dresses they had displayed in the shop. The clerk was a bit suspicious of me when I entered, but the moment I flashed my coin, he dropped his objections and was more than happy to serve me. I spoke to him in Zallabarian, and while his own grasp of the language wasn't very good, we understood enough to make a transaction.

It took a while to find what I was looking for, but eventually I walked out in a smart-looking dark grey outfit that went well with my boots and made me look more like a businesswoman.

My next stop was the stagecoach office located in the center of town. "Excuse me," I said in Zallabarian to the man standing outside a faded red coach. "I'd like to book passage to the capital."

The man narrowed his eyes at me, and I got the distinct sensation that he didn't like Zallabarians. Would I ever win? For a heart-stopping moment, I wondered if he wasn't going to accept my money.

"Very well," he finally said in Zallabarian, though he had a heavy Traggaran accent. He took my money, gave me a ticket, and stepped aside to allow me into the coach. The space was cramped, with at least ten people jammed inside, but I wasn't about to complain. It was still better than busting my feet.

The heat from all the bodies in the coach made it difficult to stay awake, but I managed to keep my eyes open the entire nine-hour drive. By the time we arrived at the capital, my lower back was cramping, and my eyes felt heavy, like they were weighed down by anvils. But one whiff of the rank air forced me wide awake again.

"Lovely," I muttered under my breath as I looked around the cobblestone streets. The smell of horse manure mixed with human urine was extremely unappealing, and the drab buildings certainly didn't make a good impression either. Hopefully this stagecoach stop was in an impoverished part of the city.

"Hey, young lady!" a male voice called. "I think you lost something!"

I turned toward the voice, and two hands clamped around my upper arms. "Hey!" I cried as I struggled against the hold of two city guards, still speaking Zallabarian. These guards were much bigger and stronger than the ones I'd evaded earlier, and the glint in their eyes was downright mean. "Unhand me at once!"

The one on my left laughed, his lip curling back into a sneer. "It's too late," he said in Elantian, and my mouth dropped open in horror as I realized my mistake—he'd called out to me in my native language, and I'd responded. "Drop the act, missy—we know you're a spy!"

"Stop! This is a mistake!" I shrieked as they dragged me to a prison wagon waiting nearby. I kicked and struggled, but I was no match for these men, and my weapons were too far away for me to reach. Stopping by the wagon, one of them wrenched my hands behind my back, and the other one patted me down, removing my weapons and gear.

"Pig," I hissed as he squeezed my ass.

He slapped my face so hard, my lower lip split open. "Shut up, whore," he spat as blood gushed down my chin. "You have no rights here." The second guard ripped my pack from my back, then tied my hands and threw me in the back of the wagon. "Enjoy the ride," he called in a mocking voice.

The wagon had no seats in the back, and smelled strongly of piss and shit. Eyes watering from the smell, I struggled to get myself upright, but the wagon lurched forward, slamming my head into the wall.

"Shit," I swore as stars swam before my eyes. I tried to get a hold of myself, but my head was spinning, my skull throbbing. Instinctively, I shut my eyes against the pain, and was immediately dragged down into unconsciousness, away from reality.

I just hoped that when I woke up, I wouldn't find a noose wrapped around my neck.

20

I woke up the next morning lying on a stone bench in a jail cell. For a long moment, I didn't move a muscle—my head and face were throbbing, every single fiber in my body strung tight as I listened to my surroundings. Off in the distance, a steady drip, drip spoke of a leak, fellow prisoners grunted and grumbled, and I even caught the faintest hint of laughter.

Carefully, I sat up to try to get a better look, and nearly fell off my chair at the sight of a man staring at me as he leaned against the opposite wall. He was huge, at least seven feet tall, dressed in a guard's uniform with a giant key ring attached to his belt. I guessed he must be the prison warden.

"Well, well," he said in a gravelly voice. "Looks like she's awake."

I lunged for the bars. "Please," I said in Traggaran, hoping I could appeal to him by speaking his native language. "This is all a big mistake. I'm not a spy, I'm a friend of—"

"Shut up." He moved toward me, and I shut my mouth instantly.

Was I light-fingered enough to steal the keys from his belt? Did I dare? "I don't care who you are, what you've done, or why you're here. My job is to make sure you stay put until the king says otherwise. We clear?"

I swallowed hard. "Crystal."

He stalked away, and I slumped back onto the bench, defeated. What should I do next? I could tell the warden didn't care what I said; he'd keep me down here until he was ordered otherwise. If someone with higher authority came to speak to me, I could invoke Tavarian's name and see if that would be enough to release me. But would that jeopardize his mission? Dammit, I didn't want to get him into trouble if there was a chance he could convince the Traggarans to stand down. But if they decided to kill me, I didn't see how I had any choice.

The warden came back a bit later with a tray of gruel, and I wolfed it down hungrily, ignoring the awful taste. For the next two days and nights I lived this way, scarfing down terrible food, relieving myself in the stinking chamber pot, and driving myself out of my mind with worry. I was too far away to communicate with Lessie now, but I could feel her concern for me in the bond. I did my best to push my thoughts toward her: that I was fine for now, and to please stay put. The last thing I needed was for her to charge in here and rescue me. All it would take was a well-placed shot with a cannon, and we would both die before I ever saw the light of day again.

On the third day, I was just starting to give up hope when the warden came up to my cell door. The sound of keys jangling got my attention, and I jumped to my feet as he opened the cell door. Two guards waited in the corridor, and though I was relieved to see neither of them was the man who groped and slapped me, I was still nervous.

"Where are you taking me?" I asked as they motioned me to step outside of the cell. I expected them to tie my wrists again, but they didn't.

"This way, my lady," one of the guards said, and I blinked. My lady? Confused, I followed them out of the dungeon and up a set of stairs. We entered a long hallway with a red carpet running down the length, embroidered with the Traggaran crest —a horned sea monster on a backdrop of waves. As we continued down a series of corridors, I squinted against the light streaming in through the windows.

The guards led me into a large room. It was well-appointed, but somewhat sparse compared to how Elantians decorated, with very little art on the walls, and shaggy furs rather than rugs covering the stone floors. Several older men in uniform stood near the giant hearth, arguing in Traggaran, and I noticed a few civilians among them too. My jaw nearly hit the floor when one of them, an older man dressed in elegant Zallabarian robes, turned to meet my gaze.

Salcombe?

"Oh, thank gods!" Salcombe cried in perfect Traggaran. "You've found her!"

"So, this is your wife, then?" one of the officers asked as Salcombe strode toward me, his face the picture of joy and relief. He was still using the fan to make himself appear as an attractive man in his forties, but I'd know him anywhere. How the hell did he end up here?

"Yes, this is my dear Zara." Salcombe drew me into his arms, and I stiffened. He immediately launched into a spate of Zallabarian, thanking providence for saving me from that awful shipwreck that had separated us. "Play along," he muttered under his breath.

Burying a wave of disgust, I forced myself to return his embrace, sobbing in relief. "I was so frightened!" I wailed dramatically, clinging to his robes. Now it was his turn to stop himself from pulling away—Salcombe loathed few things more than a hysterical woman, and he knew I was playing it up to get back at him.

"There, there," he crooned, patting my back while trying to hide his obvious discomfort. Somehow, he managed to disentangle himself from me without looking like he was trying to get away from me and turned back to the officers. "Yes, she is definitely the one," he confirmed to the others, switching back to Traggaran again.

The officers laughed at the knowing tone in his voice. "I am glad we were able to help reunite you with your wife, Lord Trentiano," one of them said. "When you gave us her description, I had the warden fetch her immediately. I am very sorry for the mix-up, Lady Trentiano."

I held the officer's gaze for a long moment, making both him and Salcombe sweat a bit. I could refute Salcombe's story right here and now, exposing him as an Elantian. But where would that get me, except thrown back into my cell?

"You are forgiven," I finally said, giving him a sweet smile. "Although I very much would like to take a bath right now."

"We'll take care of that as soon as we get you home," Salcombe said smoothly, linking his arm with mine. "Please give the king my regards," he said to the officer over his shoulders. "We are looking forward to meeting him."

Questions clamored in my mind for attention, but I held my tongue as Salcombe steered me out of the palace and into a waiting carriage. His two bodyguards, Trolbos among them, filed in with us, and tension filled the cramped space as the carriage lurched forward, rumbling toward the gates.

I held my breath until we cleared them.

"Well?" Salcombe asked, arching his eyebrows. "Aren't you going to thank me for rescuing you?"

I scowled. "If you were anyone else, I would be grateful," I said. "But I doubt you did this out of the goodness of your heart. What do you want?" Did he know about my run-in with his followers? A chill went through me. I wasn't entirely certain I hadn't killed the one man I'd sliced in the neck. What if he found out?

I expected Salcombe to snap at me, but to my surprise, he laughed. "Cynical as ever. I've taught you well. It is a good thing I still had the location spell, or you might be swinging from the gallows right now instead of standing here with me. The king is very paranoid just now, and foreigners are being snatched off the streets left, right, and center. I might have ended up in that prison too, if not for my Zallabarian papers."

242 | JESSICA DRAKE

I rolled my eyes. "Of course you would walk out of Zallabar with citizenship papers." But another thought hit me, and goosebumps raced across my flesh. If the king was throwing foreigners into prison, then what did he do with Lord Tavarian? Had he been down in that dungeon with me the entire time?

"Something wrong?" Salcombe arched a brow.

I clenched my jaw, shoving the thought away. I wouldn't believe it until I had proof. "Just the fact that I'm sitting here with you," I said coolly. "Now are you going to tell me what you're doing here?"

"Searching for relics, of course," Salcombe said with a grin. "It is fortuitous that my hunch proved right, and you were here, for I could use your skills. I have a lead on a relic not far from here that might very well be a piece of the dragon god's heart."

"And what makes you think I'll help you find it?"

"It's the least you can do after I rescued you from prison," Salcombe said. "If you're not interested, I can just use this"—he pulled the fan from his robes and dangled it in the air—"to change your face, then send you back and tell the guards you were a mage disguising yourself as my wife to try to steal my money. If there is one thing the Traggarans hate more than dragons, it's mages."

"You bastard," I hissed.

The carriage rolled to a stop in front of a townhouse, cutting off our conversation. A footman opened the door, and as he helped me down, I scanned the busy street, wondering if I should try to make a break for it.

"I took the liberty of retrieving your weapons and gear," Salcombe said silkily. He placed a hand at the small of my back and steered me toward the house, reminding me who was in charge. "I am more than happy to return them to you once we strike a proper agreement."

Dammit. It was one thing to leave my knives behind, but I couldn't abandon my lock picks or my dragon blade. I was going to have to stay until I could figure out how to get them back. If I could also steal back the hair Salcombe had taken from me, all the better.

"You sure seem to have everything figured out," I said as we stepped into a black-and-white tiled foyer.

A servant bustled over to take Salcombe's coat. "Welcome back, my lord," he said in accented Zallabarian. His blue eyes flicked over my disheveled form. "Is this your lovely wife?"

"Yes, indeed. Zara, this is Willsworth, our butler." Salcombe nudged me toward him. "Please show her to her rooms, and have a bath drawn for her. She's been through quite an ordeal, and needs her rest."

"Of course." Willsworth bowed. "Please follow me, my lady."

I thought about resisting, but the truth was I did need a bath, and I also needed time and space from Salcombe. I followed after Willsworth, who led me up a curving staircase and into a suite that would have been quite grand if not for the two goons waiting inside. Everything was done in shades of pink and white, and I was struck by the vicious urge to flop down on the settee and smear the dirt from my boots all over it. Sure, it wasn't Salcombe's furniture, but he'd still have to pay for the damage. And right now I wanted to damage him as much as I could.

Before I could act on the childish urge, several more servants bustled in, carrying buckets of water. "Oh, my lady!" a maid exclaimed, taking me by the arm. From the shock on her round, pleasant face, I could tell that I looked even worse than I smelled. "I'm so sorry for the terrible ordeal you've been through. Let's get you out of these clothes and into that bath."

I followed the maid into the bathroom, then stripped off my clothes while the servants filled the tub. Two of them offered to help me bathe, but I shooed them away as I slipped into the fragrant water. Despite my anger, despite my separation from Lessie and my forced reunion with Salcombe, I groaned with bliss as my body sank into the bath—the heat seeping into my muscles felt unbelievably good.

Tipping my head back to rest against the lip of the tub, I stared at the ceiling and contemplated my options. The irony that I was stuck with Salcombe yet again chaffed, considering I'd come here looking for help to beat him. The last thing I wanted to do was help him recover yet another piece of heart.

And yet, I had no other option but to stay, at least for now. Sticking close to him would buy me some time, give me an opportunity to figure out how to sabotage him, steal my stuff back, and find Lord Tavarian. Was Tavarian even in the palace?

And if so, did he know Salcombe had been there as well? For all I knew Tavarian had concluded his business and left already.

You'll figure this out, Zara. I had to. Lessie was out there, waiting for me, and I had to get back to her soon before she came looking for me. If the locals saw a dragon flying over the capital, they would take it as an act of war. Tavarian's mission would be compromised, and thousands of lives would be lost.

As long as there is life, there is hope, I told myself.

Now, I only had to believe it.

To be continued...

Zara and Lessie's adventures will continue in MIGHT OF THE DRAGON, Book 3 of the Dragon Riders of Elantia series! Make sure to follow the author on Amazon so you can be notified when the book is released!

Did you enjoy this book? Please consider leaving a review, even if it's just a single sentence. Reviews help authors sell books, and the better a book sells, the faster its sequel gets written. Plus, they make the author feel warm and fuzzy inside. And who doesn't want that? :)

ABOUT THE AUTHOR

JESSICA DRAKE is obsessed with books, chocolate, and traveling. When she's not binge-watching Lord of the Rings or jet-setting around the world, she can be found chained to her computer, feverishly working on her next project. She loves to hear from her readers, so feel free to drop her a line at jessica@authorjessicadrake.com.

Made in the USA
San Bernardino, CA
25 January 2019